W9-DCO-660

THE PARKER CAFE

KAY CORRELL

ZURA LU PUBLISHING, LLC

This book is dedicated to those people who love the beach. Love to hunt for seashells and sea glass. Who crave time just sitting on the beach and watching the waves roll in. You are my people.

THE PARKER CAFE

Olivia is determined to get the new cafe up and running. She just hopes she can prove to herself, her mother, and the town that she's capable of making it a successful venture.

When the charming Austin Woods comes to town and offers to help with promotion and social media, how can she refuse?

But someone returns to town and threatens to ruin everything...

Read more about the lives of the Parker Women in this delightful continuation of the Moonbeam Bay series.

Heather and Jesse are still at odds... and why is that?

Evelyn's uses her cooking talents to plan out the menu for the cafe and hopes to finally have a career she can be proud of. Donna and Barry continue on with their romance despite some road bumps along the way.

Try this feel-good beach read!

MOONBEAM BAY - the series

The Parker Women - Book One

The Parker Cafe - Book Two

A Heather Parker Original - Book Three

The Parker Family Secret - Book Four

Grace Parker's Peach Pie - Book Five

The Perks of Being a Parker - Book Six

KAY'S BOOKS

Find more information on all my books at
kaycorrell.com

COMFORT CROSSING ~ THE SERIES

The Shop on Main - Book One
The Memory Box - Book Two
The Christmas Cottage - A Holiday Novella
(Book 2.5)
The Letter - Book Three
The Christmas Scarf - A Holiday Novella
(Book 3.5)
The Magnolia Cafe - Book Four
The Unexpected Wedding - Book Five

The Wedding in the Grove - (a crossover short story between series - with Josephine and Paul from The Letter.)

LIGHTHOUSE POINT ~ THE SERIES

Wish Upon a Shell - Book One
Wedding on the Beach - Book Two
Love at the Lighthouse - Book Three
Cottage near the Point - Book Four
Return to the Island - Book Five
Bungalow by the Bay - Book Six

CHARMING INN ~ Return to Lighthouse Point

One Simple Wish - Book One
Two of a Kind - Book Two
Three Little Things - Book Three
Four Short Weeks - Book Four
Five Years or So - Book Five
Six Hours Away - Book Six
Charming Christmas - Book Seven

SWEET RIVER ~ THE SERIES

A Dream to Believe in - Book One

A Memory to Cherish - Book Two

A Song to Remember - Book Three

A Time to Forgive - Book Four

A Summer of Secrets - Book Five

A Moment in the Moonlight - Book Six

MOONBEAM BAY ~ THE SERIES (2021)

The Parker Women - Book One

The Parker Cafe - Book Two

A Heather Parker Original - Book Three

The Parker Family Secret - Book Four

Grace Parker's Peach Pie - Book Five

The Perks of Being a Parker - Book Six

INDIGO BAY ~ A multi-author sweet romance series

Sweet Days by the Bay - Kay's Complete Collection of stories in the Indigo Bay series

Or buy them separately:

Sweet Sunrise - Book Three

Sweet Holiday Memories - A short holiday story

Sweet Starlight - Book Nine

Sign up for my newsletter at my website *kaycorrell.com* to make sure you don't miss any new releases or sales.

CHAPTER 1

Olivia Foster walked arm in arm with her cousin into the lobby of The Cabot Hotel. She looked around in amazement at the grandeur. "Oh, Heather. Look at this. It's... wonderful."

"It is." Heather's awestruck voice floated through the air.

"Aunt Evelyn, everything looks so perfect." Olivia turned to her aunt. "You did a great job getting the hotel ready for the gala. It looks like we stepped onto the set of a 1920s movie."

"I just hope everything goes smoothly." Her aunt swept her gaze around the room, taking in every little detail.

"I'm sure it will. You're the best organizer in

the world, Mom." Heather hugged her mother. "Be sure and ask us if you need any help."

"I will." Evelyn hurried off to check on one of a million little things, Olivia was sure. Her aunt had organizing events down to a science.

Heather tugged on her arm. "Look at that." She tilted her head over to the edge of the lobby. "Aunt Donna is already deep in conversation with Barry. See? Looks like he's pointing out some of the things he did with the remodel. Do you think something is going on between those two?"

She glanced over at the flushed look and shy smile on her mother's face. "I think so? Maybe. She hasn't said anything to me, though. Nothing since that one date with him."

"I definitely think something is going on." Heather glanced over at the couple again.

"I hope so." Olivia started to say more but stopped as her daughter came rushing up to them, taking one swirl in front of them before stopping.

"Isn't this great? And my dress. I can't stop twirling in it." Emily grinned and spun around once more. "And the history alcove I helped set up? It looks great. I just checked it out. I'm going to mostly circulate in there. Mr. Hamilton

—Delbert—said I should answer any questions the guests have when they go in there. He said I know more about the hotel than anyone now."

"I think you do after all that research you did." Olivia nodded, pleased to see her daughter so animated and happy.

"I'll catch up with you later, then." Her emerald green dress shimmered as she sped away.

"She's really turned into a stunning young lady." Heather nodded toward Emily.

Olivia sighed. "When did she get so grown up? Wasn't she just running around with skinned knees and braids?"

"Seems like it." Heather laughed. "Though, if it makes you feel any better, sometimes I feel like *we* were just running around with skinned knees and braids, too."

"Okay, now you're making me feel old." Olivia grinned back at her cousin. Though she didn't feel old tonight. She felt like she'd stepped into some mystical other-world.

"Enough of this, let's go check out the grand ballroom. I can't wait to see what Mom's done with it." Heather took her arm as they walked across the lobby and entered through one of the many open doors to the ballroom.

"Wow." Heather stopped beside her.

Wow was right. White twinkle lights lined the edges of the ballroom and huge chandeliers glistened from the ceiling. A small band played at the far end with a dance floor spread out before it. Servers wandered around with champagne glasses on shiny silver platters. Most of the guests had come in costumes right out of the roaring twenties.

"I feel like I've stepped back in time," Heather whispered as she reached up to touch the stylish hairband that circled her forehead with a small pearl flower attached to it. She'd twisted her hair into a knot on the side.

"I feel like I'm inside some movie," Olivia whispered.

"I know. It's just... magical."

"Livy, Heather."

She spun around at the sound of their names.

"Hey, Jesse. Wow, look at you," she took in his dashing vintage attire. "You dress up pretty great."

"This is Austin Woods." Jesse gestured to the man beside him. "Friend of mine. Here on vacation."

"Nice to meet you, Austin." She smiled at the tall man standing beside Jesse.

"Nice to meet you two."

She glanced over at Heather and frowned. Her cousin looked like someone had broken the magical spell and it had disintegrated into sharp tiny bits of crystal. Olivia elbowed her. "Doesn't Jesse look great?"

Heather nodded with one slight dip of her chin toward Jesse, her face a stony look of social politeness. "Austin, nice to meet you."

At least she acknowledged Jesse's friend.

"I heard your mother was in charge of organizing the grand opening. This looks great. She did a good job." Jesse's prior warm, welcoming tone of voice now matched Heather's perfunctory expression.

"Uh, thanks. I'll tell her you said so." The words sounded awkward, standing like a barrier between all of them as Heather stood like a statue beside her.

"Mom said she went on a dinner cruise on your boat and it was wonderful." Olivia ushered the conversation along as she tried to figure out what was going on between Jesse and Heather. They used to be great friends, but now the air had turned frigid around them.

"I do like owning The Destiny. Really enjoying it. Kind of a dream of mine to be able to purchase her."

"She said you have the boat all updated, and it looks fabulous." Olivia continued talking while giving a quick eye to Heather to question what the heck was going on.

Heather ignored her.

Austin stood awkwardly at Jesse's side, glancing between Jesse and Heather. So he'd noticed the friction, too.

"I should go find Mom and see if she needs help," Heather said, still deliberately ignoring Olivia's questioning look. "Austin, great meeting you. Hope you have a nice visit." She spun around and hurried off without saying another word to any of them.

"So... what was that?" Olivia turned to Jesse with her hands on her hips.

"What was what?" His tone held way too much false innocence.

"You and Heather. The icy stares. The forced niceties. What gives?"

"I guess you'd have to ask Heather that question." He sighed. "Anyway, hope you have a nice evening. Austin, let me introduce you to some more of the townspeople here."

The two men walked away, both looking striking in their historical attire. With his quick smile and twinkling eyes, Austin seemed like the kind of guy that everyone automatically liked. Not that it mattered. She hadn't dated in forever and had no time to think about something like that now. She took one last look over at the two men, turned, and grabbed a couple of glasses of champagne from a passing server. Something was going on between Heather and Jesse, and she planned to find out what it was. She hurried off after her cousin.

DONNA HADN'T MISSED the appreciative look in Barry's eyes when she'd walked up to him this evening.

"You look stunning, Donna."

She *did* feel sensational. The long silvery gown sparkled under the lights of the chandeliers. The elbow-length gloves felt peculiar on her arms but fit in well with the theme of the evening and lent an air of elegance.

Barry looked dashing in a suit that was cut

in a throwback 1920's style. "You look pretty dapper yourself, sir."

He handed her a glass of champagne. "You have to come see what your sister has done to the grand ballroom."

She took his arm, and they walked over to the large doors lining the entrance to the ballroom. She stopped in awe just inside the room. "Oh, look. It's just *enchanting*. Evelyn did such a great job." She looked up at the massive chandeliers casting flickering light down on the crowd below. The low strains of music came from a small group at the far end of the room.

"I couldn't have done all this without her." Barry took her elbow as they walked deeper into the crowd. They stopped and chatted with people Barry knew, and she introduced him to more of the people from town who'd come to gawk at the hotel that had stood in ruin for so many years. The hotel now threw open her arms invitingly, welcoming all to see her in her new, restored glory.

Delbert Hamilton, the owner of the hotel, walked up to them. "Barry, Donna, good to see you. A fine turnout, don't you think?"

"I think Evelyn did a great job with the

invites." Barry nodded as he looked around the room.

"Not to mention the open invitation she put up on the town's website. I'm fairly certain every single person in town is here." She laughed as she glanced around the crowd and waved to Stan Winkleman, a man she'd dated a long time ago. He was here with the town's librarian, who was actually quite a good fit for him.

"I couldn't have asked for a grander opening." Delbert's face held a wide grin. That is until he glanced over toward the open doors to the ballroom and his smile faded.

"Anything wrong?" she asked.

"What? No." But his forehead creased in a slight frown before a carefully crafted smile settled on his features.

She glanced over at the door and saw what had caught his attention. Camille Montgomery. Making a grand entrance into the ballroom as she swept through the crowd, heading straight toward them.

"Camille, you're... here," Delbert said as she approached, his smile only slightly fading before he pulled it back carefully in place.

Camille Montgomery was a vision of 1920s glamour. Her black drop-waist dress clung to her every curve, and rows of fringe danced around at knee-length. "Of course I'm here for your grand opening, Delbert, honey. Don't be silly." She placed her hand possessively on Del's arm.

Donna glanced quickly at Barry. She swore Barry told her that Del and Camille had broken up. Barry silently shrugged at her unasked question.

Delbert lightly took Camille's hand off his arm. "Camille, I didn't know you were coming. I'm sorry, I have some business I need to attend to. You can keep yourself entertained, yes?"

"But Delbert..."

"Barry, Donna, enjoy yourselves." Delbert smiled at them—a genuine smile—and turned and walked away.

"Well. I never." Camille's eyes flashed. "I thought he'd get over our little spat. He always does. And he was being *so* unreasonable. I came all the way from Lighthouse Point for his little opening of this old hotel. I much prefer it when they build new hotels for the Hamilton Hotel chain. Then they can make them... well... nice. New. Modern."

"This hotel is... glorious." Donna couldn't

think of any other word to describe it. Well, maybe she could. Fabulous. Beautiful. Majestic.

Camille sniffed. "If you like... old." She whirled around, a dismissive look on her face, and stalked off toward where the mayor was chatting with a congressman.

"I thought they broke up." She stared after the woman.

"As far as I know, they have. Del did look surprised when she showed up, didn't he?"

"Unpleasantly so."

"Well, that's theirs to work out. What do you say we take a spin on that dance floor?"

"I'd love that." Because then she'd have a chance to be back in his arms. It seemed like an eternity since their first kiss.

Was that only last night?

CHAPTER 2

Heather hurried away from Livy and Austin… and Jesse. He was the last person she wanted to see tonight. Or ever, for that matter.

Though she had to admit, Livy was right. Jesse did dress up great. He looked impossibly handsome in a suit, tie, and a boater hat tilted jauntily on his head. She should have probably acknowledged his greeting with more than just a nod and not just stood there gawking at him. She frowned, hoping she'd been friendly enough to Austin. He certainly didn't need to be in the middle of her… trouble… with Jesse.

But Livy? She'd just chattered away. Like nothing was wrong. Like it wasn't a big deal to stand there talking to Jesse after what had happened between them.

Not that she'd actually *told* her cousin what had happened.

"Okay, spill it. What was going on between you and Jesse? You guys were like best friends for years." Livy appeared at her side and thrust a glass of champagne into her hand.

"I don't know what you're talking about." She blinked, wondering if she'd pulled off the lie.

"I asked Jesse, but he said to ask you. So... tell me."

She sighed. "Tonight's not the time to talk about it. Let's just enjoy ourselves. Enjoy the gala."

"But you'll tell me at Brewster's when we meet for coffee on Monday?"

"I will. I promise. But there's not much to tell." Just how she'd screwed up. But it had all been *Jesse's* fault. He'd ruined a great friendship. Anyway, it didn't really matter. They'd grown up and moved on with their lives. She was rarely back in Moonbeam anymore, so what did it matter?

She glanced over at Jesse and Austin chatting away with the owner of the marina where he kept The Destiny docked. Jesse glanced over at her, and she ducked her head, turning her back to him and acting like she was super absorbed in watching the band.

Jillian and Jackie Jenkins, their heads close together and words flowing between them, peered over at her as they approached. She swallowed a groan. Lovely, just lovely. Could this evening get any better? She glanced over at Livy, who shrugged slightly. There was no escape.

"You Parker girls all look lovely tonight," Jillian said. Or maybe it was Jackie.

"Thank you," Livy answered.

Did Livy know which twin was which? It didn't help that tonight they were dressed in matching outfits. Navy dresses with jackets over them, and each woman had a long strand of pearls draped around her neck.

"You two look festive," Heather added. Might as well be polite. Seeing Jesse shouldn't ruin her manners.

"Jackie found these dresses for us."

Okay, the one on the left had spoken, so she must be Jillian. Perfect. As long as they didn't move much.

"Your mother was in charge of this event, wasn't she? Poor thing. It probably took her mind off of... well, you know... her—" Jillian looked around, then back at them. "Her *problems*," she whispered.

"Mom's doing fine." Heather smiled broadly at the ladies. No use fueling town gossip. It looked like her parents' divorce was going to get ugly, but the town didn't need to know that.

"It's just disgraceful what your father did. Leaving her like that." Jackie shook her head.

"Oh, look. There's Mom. We should go see her." Livy placed her hand on her arm and Heather clutched it gratefully.

"Oh, yes. We should," she said as if they hadn't all walked into the gala together less than thirty minutes ago.

They hurried off toward Donna with brief parting smiles at the two women.

"Thanks," she whispered to Livy as they walked away. "They were beginning to get to me."

"They just like to gossip. Don't pay them any mind."

"I try not to."

"Anyway, we must be losing our touch. We're usually better at avoiding them." Livy grinned.

Livy was right. They did usually manage to

avoid the twins. She'd just been so engrossed in ignoring Jesse that she hadn't even seen the women coming.

They walked up to Donna and Barry, who were just coming off the dance floor. Aunt Donna's face was flushed, and her eyes sparkled. Yes, something definitely *was* going on between those two.

"Hello, girls. Are you having a good time?" Barry had a hand at Aunt Donna's elbow.

"We are." Livy nodded.

"Yes, we are," she agreed. Or at least she would be having a good time if they didn't keep running into people she didn't want to see.

DELBERT APPROACHED DONNA AND BARRY, who were chatting with Olivia and Heather. That seemed a safe group to join. He'd carefully avoided Camille as he'd circulated the room, greeting his guests.

It annoyed him that Camille had even shown up. He was certain he'd made it plain that they were taking a break. More than a break. And she'd flounced out of the hotel weeks ago saying it was over, though he knew she thought he'd apologize, even though he'd meant *every word* he'd said. She would expect him to chase after her, but that wasn't going to happen this time. It was a relief to no longer be a couple with her. He hadn't realized how much work it had taken to have a relationship with Camille, and most of the work had been on his part, not hers.

But it shouldn't have been surprising to him that she didn't want to miss an event such as the grand opening gala. She did like her events.

He glanced over and saw her talking to the CEO of the main bank in town. She always wanted to be seen with who she considered the *right* people. He was certain she'd soon hook up with someone she felt was powerful and *important* enough for her.

He sighed. She would never change, and he was glad to be free from her. Though there was the little problem of her showing up here tonight...

He pushed thoughts of Camille away for now as he stepped up to the group. "So, are you all having a good time?"

"Fabulous time." Donna smiled at him as she, too, glanced over as Camille's look-at-me laugh filtered across the distance.

Emily came rushing up to the group, stopping short of what he thought was going to be a twirl in front of them. "Oh, Delbert—hi."

"Emily, you look lovely tonight. I've heard quite a few compliments about you. You've been impressing people with your knowledge of the history of the hotel."

The girl blushed. "Thank you. I'm having the best time. People are asking me so many questions about the hotel. There's one lady who asked a bunch. She seemed really interested. And she had on the neatest dress. It was silver, covered in rows of fringe, and she had on this headpiece with a *feather* on it. So cool."

"I do love how people really got into dressing up in costume." Olivia smiled at her daughter, obviously pleased with the girl's enthusiasm.

He had to admit that Evelyn's idea of making the gala a 1920s-themed event was a splendid idea. It just added to the charm of the old hotel. He was very proud of how the renovations had turned out.

Emily continued on with her enthusiastic recounting of her night. "And this lady said she knew the hotel back from when it was open before. Oh, look. There she is." Emily waved.

He turned to see who Emily was waving to and his breath caught in his throat.

It couldn't be, could it?

But it had to be. The same emerald green eyes. The same red hair, even if it was twisted in some kind of twenties look now, instead of the shoulder-length curls he remembered.

The woman walked up to them, a warm smile on her face. "Good evening."

"I was just telling everyone about you. And your dress. I love it." Emily bubbled with excitement. "Anyway, this is my mom, Olivia, and my grandmother, Donna. And Mom's cousin, Heather. And this is Barry, he was in charge of the remodel, and this is—"

"Delbert Hamilton," the lady interrupted and smiled at him. "I'd know you anywhere."

"I thought that was you, Cassandra." He reached out and took her hands in his while strangely familiar feelings, so long forgotten —*kind of forgotten*—swept through him.

"You two know each other?" Emily asked.

"We met here at the hotel when we were young and I'd come here in the summers with my grandparents," Delbert explained. But he'd never thought he'd see her again. She looked just as lovely as ever, with a gentle charm about her and a friendly smile. His pulse quickened just like it had back when he was just a kid, which was ridiculous.

"And I looked forward to seeing him every summer. He and his grandparents were very special guests."

"Everyone, I'd like you to meet Cassandra Cabot." He turned slightly to the group, his hands still holding hers. "Oh, is it still Cabot?"

"It is." She nodded.

"Wow, an actual Cabot. That's so neat." Emily moved closer. "A real Cabot."

Cassandra laughed. "Yes, a real Cabot. And I've so missed the hotel." She turned to him. "You've done a wonderful job with her. She looks so elegant. Like she used to before... well, before she got a bit run down."

"Thank you. We tried hard to keep her as close to the original as possible."

"Delbert, there you are, honey."

He swallowed, hard, at Camille's words and turned toward the approaching woman.

Cassandra slipped her hands from his and he kept himself—just barely— from reaching out and grasping them again.

"And who is *this*?" Camille asked, casting

dagger looks at Cassandra as she sidled up to him and put her hand on his arm.

He shifted uncomfortably. "Cassandra Cabot, meet Camille Montgomery." He removed Camille's hand from his arm and took a step away from her.

"Oh, Cabot as in... well, Cabot?"

Cassandra's lips curved into a gracious smile. "Yes, as in The Cabot Hotel."

"Shame your family let it go to such ruin."

"Camille." His tone came out sharper than he intended. But maybe not.

"Well, it was a shame. But I guess when families hit hard times..." Camille shrugged.

Cassandra stood with her head held high and a gentle smile on her face. "Yes, we did have some tough times after the hurricane hit and did so much damage. It just wasn't financially prudent at the time to rebuild and reopen the hotel." Cassandra turned to him. "But I'm grateful that you bought it and restored it. She's just... magnificent. Thank you for that."

"I was grateful for the opportunity."

"I'm sure you're busy with your responsibilities with the gala. It was great to see you again, Delbert. And nice meeting all of you." Cassandra smiled her warmhearted smile once more, turned, and disappeared into the crowd.

And all he wanted to do was to chase after her. Stop her. Talk to her some more. Hear all about what she'd been doing.

"Such a shame about her family." Camille shook her head. "Some people just don't know how to hold on to their money."

He took Camille's elbow, his jaw clenched. "If you all would excuse us?" He led Camille away from the group, out of the ballroom, and into an uncrowded spot in the corner of the lobby.

"Delbert, why are you dragging me away from the party?" A smug look settled on her features. "Oh, you finally want to apologize, don't you?"

He let go of her elbow and faced her. "Camille, what are you doing here?"

"Delbert, I know you were a bit brusque with me when I last saw you. I know you're sorry and you've been busy. I assume that's why you didn't have time to come apologize before this." She flashed him a flirty smile.

A smile that did nothing for him.

"Camille, I didn't come to apologize because I have nothing to apologize for. I was under the impression we broke up." He crossed his arms.

"Don't be silly. Of course we didn't. It was just a little spat."

"Camille, it wasn't a spat, as you call it. I meant it. You talk to people like they are beneath you. You speak without thinking of the consequences of your words." He let out a long sigh. "And I get tired of making apologies for the way you act."

"How I act? *Me*? I act just fine. You're the one being ridiculous. And rude."

"Camille, let me spell this out clearly since you obviously did not get it before. I don't think we should date anymore. It's not working out. Not for me."

Her face flushed a bright red, and she jabbed a well-manicured finger at his chest. "Delbert Hamilton, you're going to regret this."

He highly doubted it. "But you understand that we're over?"

"I wouldn't take you back if you begged me to." She lifted her chin defiantly, and she swirled away from him. "You'll be sorry, Delbert. You will. But don't try to come crawling back to me." She flounced away and swept back into the ballroom.

He'd hoped she would leave the hotel so he didn't have to see her again tonight...

But at least he'd made it clear this time. He thought he'd made it clear *last time*. He let out a long breath. "Goodbye, Camille." He said the words into the empty air and hoped this time it would truly be over and she'd just... leave him alone.

And with all the problems and trouble Camille had caused over the years, why had she picked now to stir up yet more drama?

The exact moment Cassandra had dropped back into his life.

CHAPTER 3

L ater that evening Olivia and Heather strolled through the pathways of the large garden outside the hotel. They finally sat on one of the many benches, and Olivia kicked off her shoes, rubbing her feet. "Okay, I think these outfits look smashing, but my feet. These shoes. Ugh."

"That's because you're a barefoot woman at heart." Heather laughed.

"I am. I admit it."

"Mom did an outstanding job with the gala, didn't she?"

"She sure did. She should be so proud. And now... she's moving on to becoming the cook at the cafe."

"You know, you're going to have to name the cafe." Heather eyed her.

"I know. I just can't come up with a good name." She sighed. "Moonbeam Cafe, Sunny Cafe, Magnolia Cafe. Or maybe diner... but I think it's going to be more a cafe, right? I thought of some clever names, but they don't sound right. I even tried an online generator for names. Still, nothing."

"You know the entire town is just going to call it Parker's Cafe, no matter what you name it." Heather shrugged. "But I still think you need a name."

Olivia grinned. "You're so right. Why am I over-thinking this? Parker's Cafe it is."

"No, name it something that's all yours," Heather insisted. "You could call it Livy's Place or Livy's Cafe."

"I don't know."

"Let me think of all the things you like. Things that are you." Heather frowned but it quickly turned into a grin. She snapped her fingers. "I've got it. Sea Glass Cafe."

"Because of my obsession for sea glass?"

"Exactly. And it's a cute name. Who doesn't love sea glass?"

"Sea Glass Cafe..." She rolled the name

around in her head. "You know. I like it. Like it a lot."

"Perfect. Sea Glass Cafe it is."

"People are still going to call it Parker's." Olivia sighed.

"Some will. But it won't matter. It's officially Sea Glass Cafe."

With that decided, Olivia slid her shoes back on. "I guess I should go back inside and check on Emily."

"She's probably still twirling around in her dress." Heather's lips curved into a grin of amusement.

Olivia glanced down the pathway and saw two men walking toward them. As they passed under a lamppost, she grabbed Heather's arm. "I know you haven't told me what went on with Jesse, but don't look now. He and Austin are headed our way."

Heather glanced in the direction she nodded, then looked wildly for an escape route. But short of jumping up and running, there was no avoiding the men.

Heather let out a long sigh. "Just what I need."

Jesse stopped in front of them. "Ah, the Parker women again."

"Parker women? Are you two sisters?" Austin asked, his warm smile still evident. And did he have a dimple? He did. But just one.

"Cousins," Olivia replied. "And not Parkers really. We're just descendants of Grace Parker. I'm Livy Foster, and this is Heather Carlson. The Parker thing is just... well, a town thing."

"I see." Though he didn't look like he saw...

"Actually, I *am* Heather Parker." Heather rose from the bench, her tone a bit defiant as she faced off with Jesse.

Olivia jumped up and eyed her cousin. "What?"

"Yes, she legally changed her name. Didn't she tell you?" Jesse asked, his eyes clouding with... something. Displeasure? Accusation? ... or hurt?

Olivia turned to face Heather. "What's this?"

"I just... well, since I was using Parker with my art... Heather Parker... it just seemed... easier."

"And Heather likes things easy." Jesse's tone was almost mocking.

Olivia stared at Heather, then Jesse, then back at Heather. "I... didn't know. Does Aunt Evelyn know?"

"Um... not yet." Heather shook her head.

"How long... oh, never mind. We'll talk later." Olivia wasn't sure if she was more surprised or hurt that she didn't know this huge fact about her cousin. She turned to the man standing beside Jesse. "Sorry about all this. Anyway, we come from a line of Parkers. Grace Parker and her husband opened Parker's General Store years and years ago. The town has just always called us—and our mothers— the Parker women." She shrugged, trying to make it sound like it was no big deal that her cousin hadn't bothered to tell her that she'd changed her legal name.

And why did Jesse know this, but she didn't?

Jesse took a long look at Heather, then turned to Austin. "Livy works at Parker's with her mother. And Heather is, as she said, an artist."

Olivia decided to jump in and change the subject and sort through her feelings about Heather's secret later. It appeared her cousin had been keeping lots of secrets. She turned to Austin. "So, are you enjoying your vacation?"

"It was a vacation until I got a look at Jesse's online presence for The Destiny. Crummy website. He's not even on TalkTime.

He needs to be. People go there to find places."

"Austin here is a social media guru. He has his own advising company." Jesse nodded toward his friend.

"You advise people about their social media presence?" Olivia frowned. "That's a thing? A job advising people about it?"

"Mostly companies, but some people. Influencers," Austin explained.

"I just like to skipper my boat, serve good food, and... well, I haven't done much online, I admit." Jesse shrugged.

"But that's changing. I'm going to get him all set up while I'm here."

"Hey, maybe you could help Livy with Parker's," Jesse suggested. "She's opening a new cafe there. They've expanded."

"Oh, I don't want to bother Austin on his vacation." He'd find out that she had an even worse online presence than Jesse's.

Austin laughed. "I've already figured out I'm not much of a vacation person. I wouldn't mind stopping by and I could give you some suggestions."

"I don't know. Our budget is pretty tight with the expansion."

"Free advice."

Jesse elbowed him. "Hey, at least ask for one of their ice cream sundaes in return. Best you've ever tasted."

Austin's eyes twinkled. "I can be bought with ice cream."

"Well, thank you." It did intrigue her to see what Austin could do, but she hated to impose.

"I'll come by one day this week?"

"That sounds great. I'm always there. Just ask for me."

"We're headed back inside to the gala. You ladies headed that way, too?" Austin asked.

"Yes," Olivia said.

"No," Heather said.

Olivia looked at her cousin and raised an eyebrow.

"We're just going to sit outside here for a bit longer. It got kind of noisy and crowded in there," Heather insisted.

She frowned at Heather. "I have to go find Emily."

"I think I'll just sit here a bit," Heather said emphatically.

"Alone?"

"I'll be fine."

Of course, she'd be fine. It was Moonbeam

after all. But still. She didn't like leaving her sitting out here alone.

Jesse looked at Heather and rolled his eyes. "Come on, Liv, you can walk in with us."

"I'll meet you inside later?" Olivia said as Heather deliberately sat down on the bench.

"Yes, I'll catch up with you soon."

Olivia headed back inside, dwarfed between the two tall men. She gave one last glance over her shoulder at her cousin. Jesse caught her looking back and just shrugged.

OLIVIA ENTERED the grand ballroom with Austin and Jesse, searching the crowd for a sign of Emily.

"So, you're looking for an Emily, you said?" Austin asked, then turned to Jesse. "Did I meet her? I must have met hundreds of people tonight. Jesse knows everyone."

"Olivia's daughter. You met her. When we checked out the history alcove."

"Ah, the young girl with the green dress and red hair. Yes."

"Oh, could you two excuse me for a minute? I see Mr. Jeffers over there. I need to talk to him for a minute about the rehearsal dinner cruise for his son and his son's fiancée next week."

"Sure, I'll help Livy look for her daughter."

Jesse walked away, and she and Austin stood awkwardly at the edge of the ballroom.

"So... I guess I should look in the alcove. She's probably there explaining all about the hotel's history to anyone who will listen."

"Actually, I think she's headed our way." Austin pointed through the crowd. "Isn't that her?"

Emily rushed up to them. "Mom, there you are. Are we still going to stay longer? Please? There are still so many people coming by the alcove. I want to stay there and talk with them."

"Yes, we can stay longer."

"Thanks, Mom. You're the best."

"Emily, did you meet Mr. Woods? Austin, this is Emily, my daughter."

"I did. I *think*. I met a lot of people." Emily laughed.

An infectious grin spread over Austin's face. "I know the feeling. I've met so many people tonight. You have the advantage of at least knowing the townspeople."

"And I think everyone in town came tonight." Emily's eyes shone with excitement.

Her daughter would remember this night forever.

"I'll see you later, Mom." Emily turned and took a few steps before twirling back toward them. "Oh, bye, Mr. Woods."

"Good night, Emily." Austin smiled easily and turned to her. "Your daughter is charming."

"She's... well, I think she's very special. She helped put together the history alcove for the hotel. She's quite the history buff."

Austin glanced around the crowd. "So, if you're staying for a bit, would you like another glass of champagne?"

"I do think I'd like that."

He snagged two glasses from a passing server and raised his. "To meeting new people."

"Lots of them." She laughed as they touched glasses. "I could introduce you to some more if you'd like."

"I think I've hit my limit. I hope no one expects me to remember their names."

"Like mine?" she teased.

"Livy. I've got that one." He rewarded her with a wide grin.

And his eyes twinkled. But maybe that was just the lighting in here? She tore her gaze from his face. "So, have you been to Moonbeam before?"

"Nope, first time. I needed to get away for a bit and decided to come here and look up Jesse. He offered to let me stay with him at his cottage."

"He still has that cottage over on the beach, doesn't he?"

"He does. Great view. Do you live on the beach?"

"No, I have a house on the canal system. Complete with an old boat that we putter around in."

"Many talents, I guess. You run a store and you're a boater."

"Technically, Mom runs the store and I work for her. But we expanded this year and I'm opening a small cafe. Sea Glass Cafe." It still seemed a bit strange to call it that, but she loved the name. "Should be open in a few weeks. Heather's mom, my aunt, is going to be the cook there. She's a talented chef."

"The one Jesse mentioned who organized this gala?"

"The same one."

"Looks like all you... *Parker women...* have

your talents." He winked. "See, I'm learning the local lingo."

She smiled at his reference to Parker women, but it just brought up the fact she hadn't known that Heather had legally changed her last name. She knew Heather had always clashed with her father, but was that why?

Heather—of the legal Heather Parker name—appeared at her side as if by magic. "Livy, I think I'm going to leave and walk back to my condo."

"Really? Already?"

"I'm tired. It's a nice night, I'll just walk home."

"You sure?"

"I'm certain." Her cousin gave her a quick hug and disappeared into the crowd.

Olivia frowned. She was going to pin her down for answers on Monday.

"So... Heather and Jesse. Is there something going on there?" Austin asked.

"You noticed it, too?"

"They seemed a bit... ah... cold to each other. *Deliberately* cold. And Jesse is normally the friendliest guy I know."

"I don't know what's going on. They've been friends forever. Since grade school days. But something must have happened because she hasn't gone to see him the last few times she's been in town."

"She doesn't live here?"

Olivia shook her head. "She has a condo here but travels a lot. Says it gives her inspiration for her art." She didn't want to tell him what the real reason was. Heather liked to avoid her family. At least until this whole messy divorce thing came up. Now Heather was staying in town for a while to support her mom.

"Oh, Olivia, dear." She grimaced as she recognized the voice, plastered on a polite face, and turned around to see Jackie and Jillian standing there.

"Who is this nice young man you're here with?" one of the twins asked. Would she ever figure out who was who?

"Oh, I'm not here with him. I just... I mean..."

Austin held out a hand. "Hello, I'm Austin. A friend of Jesse Brown's."

"Nice to meet you, young man. We're Jackie and Jillian," the other twin said as she shook Austin's hand. But which one was *she*?

"Olivia here is single, you know," the first twin said.

Olivia blushed and glanced at Austin.

"Is she now?" His eyes twinkled. Again. "Good to know."

"Oh, look, Austin. There's Jesse. We should catch up to him." Anything to get away from the twins and any gossip they'd come up with.

"Yes, we should." He took her arm. "Ladies, nice to meet you."

He led her away toward Jesse and she let out a sigh. "By tomorrow the whole town will think we're a couple. Mark my words."

He grinned at her. "I'd have no problem playing along with that."

She glanced up at him. And just what did he mean by that?

CHAPTER 4

Donna glanced at her watch late that evening after dropping the rest of the Parker women at their homes after the gala. A faint knock came from the front door.

At this hour?

She peeked out the window and smiled.

Barry.

She hurried to open the door.

"I hope it's not too late. I saw you come home and... I'm a bit wired from the gala. Thought you might be too?"

"Come in. How about I make us some chamomile tea?"

"That sounds wonderful, but first—" He stepped inside, took her hand, and drew her close. "I've been wanting to kiss you all night." He leaned down and kissed her gently.

She wound her arms around his neck, holding him close to her. Her pulse raced through her, warming her. Her breath came in jagged little sips for oxygen. He finally stopped kissing her and she leaned against him, feeling his heartbeat. Her heart pounded against his.

"Now, I guess if I can get up the willpower to let you go, we could have the tea."

She laughed softly. "Yes, in a minute."

He held her tightly. "You feel very nice in my arms."

She circled her arms around his waist, pulling closer. It did feel nice just encircled in his strong arms, in the stillness of the night. The stillness that was so welcome after the noise and hubbub of the gala.

She reluctantly pulled away from him. "Let me put the teakettle on. I'll make tea and we can go sit out on the point. Look at the stars. Unwind a bit."

"Sounds great."

The familiar actions of making the tea comforted her, and she did the steps automatically while he lounged against the counter. They took their tea outside and settled in the Adirondack chairs.

"Ah, this is nice." Barry stretched out his long legs. He still had on part of his gala outfit, but he'd lost the jacket, tie, and his shoes. She smiled at the eclectic mixture of dressed up and casual.

She set her tea on the side table and pulled off her shoes. "Ah, that's better."

"I lost mine the minute I walked in the door to my house tonight. We must have stood for hours at the gala."

"We did. But I had a fabulous time. And Evelyn was thrilled everything turned out so nice."

"She did an excellent job."

She picked up her cup and took a sip of the soothing brew, then turned to him. "What do you think was going on between Delbert and Camille?"

"I have no idea. He said they'd broken up. But she sure wasn't acting that way."

"But did you see her after Delbert led her out of the ballroom? She came back later and wow, did she look angry. And she was flirting outrageously with every man she talked to after that."

"I'm pretty sure it's over between them. At least in Delbert's view."

"Ah, well, I probably shouldn't be gossiping about it, anyway." She shook her head. She was no fan of Camille's, but still it didn't feel right to gossip about her. "But that Cassandra Cabot woman was fascinating, wasn't she?"

"She was charming."

"So fun that she and Del knew each other from when they were young." She paused, wondering if she should add her thoughts.

A soft laugh escaped Barry. "Go ahead. I can see you want to add something."

She smiled at him in the soft glow of the fairy lights from the solar mason jars scattered around them. "Well... I thought Del looked at Cassandra like... well, as if he *liked* her. Some kind of longing in his eyes."

"I don't know. They haven't seen each other in years."

"I know, but still... I think there was some spark between them. And her eyes lit up when she saw *him*. I just think..." She sighed. "Oh, I'm just a hopeless romantic, I guess. But it's probably a moot point since she was just here to see the hotel. Wonder where she lives now?"

"No clue. She hurried off after Camille

came up and started acting all possessive of Delbert."

"Yes, that was awkward."

"You know what else was awkward?" Barry asked.

She frowned. "No, what?"

"The fact I wanted to pull you into a dark corner and kiss you all night long. What would the Parker women have thought about that?"

"What the Parker women don't know won't hurt them." She grinned at him.

They settled back in their chairs, under the moonlight, and talked or sat silent as the mood struck them. It was way into the early hours of the morning before he finally walked back home.

She slowly went to her room and took one more look at the lovely gown before slipping it off and carefully placing it back on a hanger. The night had been magical. Both the gala and the late-night visit with Barry out under the stars.

Real life was going to feel kind of... *real...* after tonight.

CHAPTER 5

On Monday morning Heather hurried down the pier toward Brewster's. She ducked down between two buildings to the back walkway when she spied Jillian and Jackie sitting on the bench in the middle of the wharf. Best to avoid them. Always the best choice.

She walked into Brewster's and spotted Livy already sitting at a table by the water. She slid onto the chair across from her and reached for the waiting coffee. After one sip, she leaned back in her chair, knowing what was coming.

Livy didn't disappoint. "Okay, so... what's the deal between you and Jesse?"

"Can't I even have my coffee first?" Heather asked, averting her eyes.

"Nope. A deal's a deal. You promised you'd tell me."

She let out a long sigh, knowing that she couldn't avoid the conversation forever. "There isn't much to tell. He made a mistake, and I reacted badly to it. Then later he tried to apologize and... well, I didn't want to hear it." That was the short version, anyway.

"What mistake did he make?" Livy peered over her coffee mug, her eyebrow raised.

She let out yet another sigh. "He... He kissed me."

"He *kissed* you? That was the big mistake?" Livy's eyes widened.

Heather looked up, her voice firm. "Yes, it was a mistake. We were friends. Like forever. He was easy to be with. Fun to talk to. I loved being his friend. But he ruined everything when he kissed me."

Livy frowned. "And how did you react badly?"

"I..." She broke into a sheepish grin and shrugged. "I slapped him."

"You *slapped* him?" Livy tried hard to squelch her laughter but failed. Miserably.

"Yes, he just surprised me and all I could think was that he was ruining everything."

"And you told him that?"

"I did. I said he'd ruined everything and how our friendship was wrecked and..."

"And what is it that you're not telling me?" Livy looked unconvinced.

Heather paused, trying to decide how to explain everything that had happened. "After I turned and stalked away self-righteously... Because I was *sure* I was right. Then I realized..." Heather gazed down, then finally looked back up. "I realized I *liked* his kiss."

"So you apologized, right?" Livy leaned forward. "Right?"

"No... Well, I tried. I did. I went to go see him the next time I was in town. After I sorted things out in my mind. It was months later. We talked some." Actually, they'd talked for hours, all night and into the early morning, and she was certain that things would get back on track for them.

"So why are things still so wrong between the two of you?"

"I thought we were back on even footing after our... talk. But then I went to go see him the next night and he had a girl at his cottage. That Shelly Newson."

"He's allowed to date. Especially since you shut him down pretty firmly with that slap."

"I know... but he couldn't get me away fast enough when Shelly was there. It was awkward, so I just left."

"And that's how you left it?"

"Actually, he came to my condo a few days later. I let him in... and he saw some things I had spread out on the table. The paperwork to change my name to Parker. He asked what that was about. So I told him I was legally changing my last name."

"Okay, so that's why he knew about the Parker name and I didn't—and we'll talk about that in a minute—so you talked it out when he came over. This time Shelly wasn't around, so you sorted it out?"

"Not exactly."

"How not exactly?"

"He saw the papers and jumped on it. Thought that legally changing my name was going too far. That it would hurt Mom's feelings. That I didn't need to do that to distance myself from my father."

"He's right on that. You could avoid your dad without changing your name. *Did* you change it to get back at your father?"

"Maybe a little. He never acted like he wanted me to be his daughter. Then after using Heather Parker as my artist name... it just seemed easier."

"He was probably right about your mom. It will hurt her feelings. Or it *would* have hurt her feelings. Maybe not now—now that your father is divorcing her."

"Anyway, I didn't take the criticism —constructive or not—very well. I kicked him out. I mean, it's not his decision on what my name is." Though, that hadn't been the real reason she'd kicked him out. She'd still been smarting from how he'd been so eager to get rid of her when Shelly was at his cottage.

Livy frowned. "No, it's not his decision to make. But he was probably just wanting you to consider your options. You know Jesse, he thinks things through from every angle. Over analyzes. Always has."

"You're right. He does. But... I've had a lot of years of running my life exactly as I see fit. I don't need anyone controlling my life like my father did. The constant criticism. Never living up to expectations. I don't like to be told what to do."

"But Jesse's not like that." Livy's eyes held a

glint of skepticism.

"No, Jesse's not like my father." Heather sighed. How many times had she sighed this morning? "And he did see me later and apologized for stepping in with his opinion. But really, by then things were strained between us. Then I ran into him again, talking with Shelly on the wharf. They were in an intense conversation, and I figured it was better if I just let things go."

"Sounds like just one big misunderstanding to me." Livy shook her head. "Why don't you try talking to him again?"

"Because..." Heather set down her coffee. It was all so complicated to explain. "Because even though I said *he* ruined things, I really think it was me. *I* ruined things. But anyway... if he wants more than friendship, I don't think I can give him that."

"Maybe he'd be fine with being friends again."

"Maybe."

"*Maybe* you should stop being so stubborn. Go talk to him."

"He is dating Shelly now, isn't he?" Heather asked, uncertain if she really wanted to know the answer.

"I've seen them together a few times. Not often."

She shrugged. "Maybe things are just better like they are. We grow up. Grow apart."

"Maybe, maybe, maybe. I still think you should try talking to him. He's a good guy. He was a good friend to you. You could sort things out."

"I don't know." And frankly, the best thing she could do at this stage was just to stay far away from him. For her sake, for his sake, for her heart's sake.

"Will you at least think about it?" Livy wouldn't let it go.

"Sure." But she was certain her expression didn't look the least bit convincing.

Livy took a sip of her coffee and set the mug down. "Now, about the Parker thing. Why didn't you tell me you legally changed your name?"

"I was afraid you'd be mad. Or tell me I was doing the wrong thing."

"I've always supported your decisions." Livy reached over and took her hand.

"I know. It was just easier if no one knew. If I didn't have to explain myself. If... Mother didn't find out."

"You know I'll always be there for you. No

more secrets. Not about names. Not about Jesse. I hate feeling like we're growing apart."

Heather squeezed her hand. "We're not growing apart. I was just being... foolish. I should have told you about the name and about Jesse. But you've just been so busy these last few years and I didn't want to add to everything you have to worry about." Heather shrugged.

"I'm never too busy for you, Heather. Never. No more secrets." Livy looked directly at her.

"No more." And just like that, she lied to her cousin. A lie of omission, but still a lie.

Livy finished her coffee and left to go work at Parker's. Heather stayed at Brewster's and sipped on a second cup of coffee.

No more secrets. Wasn't that just one big lie?

It was technically a good plan. Best friends shouldn't keep secrets from each other. Especially after promising not to.

But she hadn't actually explained the timeline between her and Jesse exactly right. She'd left out a few details. Big details. Details going back to when they were young.

So, no more secrets except...

... she still had one more secret that she didn't plan to tell anyone. Not even Livy.

CHAPTER 6

L ivy turned around at the sound of the door opening to the cafe. The cafe that *still* wasn't opened yet, and the sign plastered on the door clearly stated the fact. Her ire tempered, though, when she saw it was Austin. "Good morning."

"I can read, really. The sign says you're not open. But I did say I'd come by and see you."

"No, come in. I'm waiting for the electrician who's going to get the soda fountain all wired up. He already finished in the kitchen, and Aunt Evelyn should be here soon to get it all organized just like she wants it."

"When do you plan to open?" He glanced around the cafe.

"In about two weeks. Or I hope so."

"Are you having a grand opening?"

She laughed. "Like the gala for The Cabot Hotel grand opening? I don't think so."

"But you could get some good PR from having an official grand opening. Did you list it as coming soon on your TalkTime page?"

"So would you believe me if I said we don't have one?"

He laughed. "I'd believe you. Jesse didn't either until I sat down with him and set one up. Do you want me to do that with you?"

"I can't pay you in ice cream sundaes yet. No ice cream until Evelyn orders in all the supplies and gets us started again."

"I'm fine with delayed gratification." He grinned a boyish smile. "Come on. Let me show you. Want to use a laptop or phone?"

"Laptop might be easier. I'm all thumbs at typing on my phone. Let me go get it." She returned with her laptop and they sat at one of the cafe tables.

"No page for Parker's General Store, either?"

"Nope."

"Do you want to be part of the Parker's General Store page or a separate page?"

She'd love to say separate. To keep the cafe

her own thing. The first thing at Parker's her mother had let her be totally in charge of. But it didn't make good business sense, did it? The town would see it as an extension of Parker's General Store.

"I guess with the main store." At least it would have its own name.

"We could set it up as a separate page and just link the two together."

"Okay, that sounds good." The small act of having her own page for Sea Glass Cafe pleased her. Probably more than it should. She just wanted the cafe to be all hers. And prove she could make it a success...

He asked her questions and filled out the fields on the laptop. Before long they had a Parker's page on TalkTime. Complete with really decent photos of the front of the general store that he took on his way-newer and fancier phone.

"Now, we're going to do some posts about the expansion. The new cafe. Sea Glass Cafe, right? We'll set up the cafe's page."

"Yes, Sea Glass Cafe. Though most of the town will probably call it Parker's cafe. I have a sign guy coming to give me a quote for putting the name in the front window." Maybe with the sign in the window and the name of Sea Glass Cafe on the menus she'd have some chance of convincing the town to call it that.

"Sea Glass Cafe it is. I like that. Let me go get a photo of the front door and window of the cafe."

He came back in with Emily at his side. "Wow, Mom, Mr. Woods just told me that you're making a page for Parker's and one for the cafe. About time. Welcome to this century." Emily plopped down beside her and swiveled the laptop so she could see the screen. "Let me see them."

Austin pulled up the photo he'd just taken.

"Can you send that to me?" Emily asked. "I'll add coming soon to it. We'll upload it to the page."

"You know how to do all this?" She eyed her daughter.

"Of course, Mom. Just because you don't do social media doesn't mean I don't."

"The page has to be kept updated. Post to it often. List sales. Maybe your daily special at the cafe. Things like that," Austin said as he sat on the other side of her.

"I can do that, Mom. Let me be in charge

of it!" An eager look settled in Emily's eyes. "Please?"

"You sure? You're already busy with school and other work here at Parker's."

"Yes, I'd love to."

"Then the job is yours."

"Perfect. I'm going to post this photo to the page now. Do you have an official opening date?"

"Wow, you and Austin. Thinking alike. No, but I'm hoping in a couple of weeks."

"I need the login info."

Austin gave it to Emily, and she typed away on her phone.

"There, I'm in. And we should have a grand opening," Emily said as she kept typing away.

She narrowed her eyes at Emily, then Austin. "Have you two been talking?"

Emily looked up. "What? No, why?"

"Austin said the same thing. Said it was good marketing to hype an opening."

"It sure worked for the hotel. Did you see how many people were there? And Delbert said they're almost full of reservations for the month. I think everyone wants to go stay there and see it now that it's all fixed up."

"I'll talk to Evelyn and see how much time

she needs, then we'll pick an opening date." She chewed on her lip. She was anxious to open, but nervous. What if she'd made the wrong decision? What if the cafe wasn't a success? Heather had invested in it. What if she lost all her cousin's money?

"You okay?" Austin asked.

"Sure." She tried to look convincing.

"You look… concerned."

She smiled weakly. "Just a lot of things to juggle at once."

Emily jumped up. "I've gotta run. But don't worry about the page, Mom. I've got it." She turned to Austin. "I don't suppose you can talk her into updating the website while you're at it?"

"I make no promises," Austin laughed.

"It looks like it was made in 1990… and it probably was." Emily hurried out of the cafe.

Austin leaned forward on the table. "There are a lot of balls to juggle with owning and running a business, aren't there?"

"There sure are. I mean, I love the challenge. I've really enjoyed coordinating the expansion and setting up the cafe. I just—" She stopped, unwilling to tell him—an almost-stranger—that she was worried she'd fail. That the cafe would flop. That the decision to expand had been a bad one.

"Just what?"

"I just want things to go well." She'd leave it at that.

"So, pick an opening date. Let's update your website. Is it search engine optimized?"

She was sure her eyes glazed over. "Um... probably not."

"How about I take a look at it? I could help with it."

"I can't ask you to help with all of this. You're supposed to be on vacation."

He grinned. "This *is* vacation for me. I'm not really a kick back and do nothing type guy. And I love doing this stuff. At least let me look at it."

She pushed the laptop toward him. "Have a look." She stood and nodded toward the door. "There's the electrician. Let me get him started."

Once she got the electrician set up, Evelyn came in. They discussed what Evelyn should work on first, and Olivia left her busy making a list of supplies to order.

She finally came back to sit beside Austin. "Sorry, I didn't mean for that to take that long."

"No problem. Gave me time to dig through your website. You do need to update it. You know, you could also put in an online ordering system for the cafe. People might like to order sandwiches or whatever to pick up."

She shoved her hair back from her face. "That's a good idea... yet one more thing to learn. And software to buy, I assume."

"I could set it up and show you how it works."

"Could you give me a quote for doing that?" She didn't know where she'd find the money, though. She'd just about tapped out everything she had. And there was no way she'd touch Emily's college money. Her mother hadn't been overly excited about the expansion, so she didn't want to ask her.

"I will." He pushed back from the table and shut the laptop. "Now, there's something else I wanted to ask."

"What's that?" She frowned.

"So I ran into those ladies. The twins? Jackie, Jennifer, Judy? You know, the ones with the J names."

"Jackie and Jillian."

He nodded. "Apparently when I said I was headed to the cafe, it cemented the fact that you and I are an item." He grinned. "So if the rumor about us is true, that we're dating, would you like to go out with me? Dinner?"

"I... uh..." She hadn't been expecting *that* question. And here he was giving her all this help. She couldn't turn him down, could she? She bit her lower lip. Did she want to go out with him? Dating had been the furthest thing from her mind for ages. But now... what could one little date hurt?

"I can see your mind racing. It's okay if you don't want to. I just thought—" His smile dimmed.

"No, I'd love to."

"Excellent. When? My schedule is wide open."

"Wednesday night?" She'd have to wrap up early here, and she was crazy busy, but a night off with just adult conversation and no spreadsheets sounded pretty darn good to her.

"Wednesday it is. Where would you like to go?"

"If you don't mind casual, I love going to Jimmy's out on the end of the wharf. It's right on the water. They usually have some kind of live music."

"Sounds great. Can I pick you up? Here? Or at your house?"

"How about I just meet you there?" She wasn't sure she wanted Emily to know she was going out, though she wasn't planning on hiding it. Not exactly.

"I can do that." He stood. "And I'll get you that quote you asked for."

"Thanks, Austin. For everything you did today. For your help."

"My pleasure." He crossed the floor with long strides and disappeared out the door.

She sat and stared at the door after he left. A date. Was she ready for a date? Her life was so impossibly busy now with the cafe, the expansion of Parker's, and Emily.

She pushed up from the table. But it was one little date. What could it hurt?

CHAPTER 7

That evening Austin sat with Jesse on the wide porch of The Cabot Hotel. A breeze pushed the humidity away, and they sat overlooking the bay, watching the boats sail past. They'd both grabbed beers at the bar and had come outside to enjoy the view. Austin leaned back in the Adirondack chair—surprisingly comfortable—and stretched out his legs. "This is nice."

"It is. We have a few bars here in Moonbeam, but sitting outside like this is more... peaceful. And since I didn't have a dinner cruise tonight, it's nice to take a little break." Jesse took a sip of beer. "So, did you help Livy today?"

"I did. We set up a TalkTime page for Parker's and one for Sea Glass Cafe."

"Oh, she decided on a name for the cafe, huh?"

"She did. But she swears the town will call it Parker's Cafe."

Jesse grinned. "She's probably right."

"And she wants a quote for me doing some work on her website. Update it. Possibly set up an online ordering system." He frowned. "But I get the impression she doesn't have much cash to spend."

"Probably not. I'm sure they sank a bunch into the expansion."

"I'd do it for free if she'd let me." He shrugged. "I've got the time."

"You always were the helper person." Jesse shook his head. "I think you volunteered for just about everything in college. I doubt if she'll let you do it for free, though."

"Never hurts to help people."

"No, it doesn't." Jesse nodded.

"Mr. Woods, I saw you come in. Hi, Jesse." Emily hurried up to them.

"How come Jesse is Jesse, and I'm Mr. Woods?" Austin asked, smiling at the girl.

"I don't know..." Emily shrugged. "'Cause I just met you?"

"So, you'll call me Austin, right?"

"If you want me to... Austin." She nodded. "Anyway, I was talking to Delbert—you know him? He owns the hotel. Telling him about how you set up the page for Parker's General Store and were working on our social presence. He wants to talk to you. Oh, look, here he is."

Austin rose as the man approached.

"Delbert, this is Mr. Woods. I mean, Austin. Austin, this is Delbert Hamilton."

Austin reached out his hand. "Pleased to meet you."

"Likewise." Delbert's firm grip surrounded his hand. "So, I admit, I did a bit of research on you after Emily talked to me earlier today. Impressive resume of companies you've worked with. Called a few CEOs I knew from companies you've worked with. Glowing reviews of your work. Could we talk about you updating The Cabot Hotel's online presence? And possibly the Hamilton Hotel's main site?"

Surprise tinged with pride swept through him at hearing Del's compliments. "Yes, sir. I'd love to discuss what you want and quote you on that."

"I understand you're here on vacation. We could talk after your vacation."

Austin laughed. "It appears I'm not very good at the whole vacation thing. I thrive on work. I could set up a time to talk to you later this week."

"That would be perfect. Where are you staying?"

"I'm staying with Jesse, but I'm afraid I'm going to wear out my welcome. Might look for a place to rent for a bit. It seems I'm picking up quite a bit of work here in the area."

"You don't have to leave my place. Plenty of room," Jesse said.

"Thanks, Jesse, but I know you weren't planning on a long-term houseguest." Austin turned back to Delbert. "So what did you have in mind for changes?"

"I'm hoping to update our page. Get events listed. Probably list some of the history of the hotel."

"It will need to be updated regularly. That's part of the success with social media."

"Oh, I could help with that. I'm going to do it for Parker's." Emily's face was the picture of wide-eyed hope, and she bounced on her toes with such anticipation that he thought she might spontaneously twirl the way she had at the gala.

"I could show her how to do it. What needs to be done. Set her up with a content schedule." Austin eyed the girl. She was eager to learn. And he'd seen how quickly she'd uploaded the photo for the cafe—complete with a text overlay that made it look like the Sea Glass Cafe sign was already in place.

"That sounds good. Emily did excellent work for us setting up the history alcove. She's an industrious worker." Delbert nodded.

"Thanks, Delbert. You won't regret this." Emily practically danced on the wide wooden porch planks.

"I'll call you in the morning to set up a time later this week to meet. Give me a bit of time to see what you currently have going online." Austin's mind was already reeling with ideas. He loved what he did. Helping companies and people get a handle on social media and their online presence.

"Sounds good. I'll leave you to enjoy your happy hour." Delbert turned and disappeared inside.

Emily grinned. "I can't wait to tell Mom. This is so cool. I'm getting the best jobs ever.

And thanks, Austin. I can't wait to learn everything that you can teach me. But I better go. Don't want to be late. We're having dinner with Grams tonight." She turned with a quick wave and hurried off.

"That girl is... energetic." Austin laughed.

"Just like her mother at that age."

"So, you've known Livy a long time?" Austin settled back in his chair.

"Forever."

"So, what's the deal with Emily's father?"

"Brett? He's pretty much out of the picture." Jesse looked out at the bay, then back at him. "He's a decent enough guy. Met him once or twice. He was just wrong for Livy. They were both young and..." He shrugged. "We all make unexpected choices when we're young. But one thing was clear. Livy always wanted Emily. And you'll never hear her say that having her was a mistake. She's a great mom."

He sat and sipped his beer, pondering his newfound information.

"Why all the questions?" Jesse interrupted his thoughts.

"I asked Livy out. We're going to dinner Wednesday. Some place called Jimmy's."

"Are you?" Jesse raised an eyebrow.

"Is that a problem?"

"No, not a problem. She just rarely dates anyone."

"She said yes to going out with me."

"Fine. But one thing."

Austin eyed him.

"Don't mess with her. She's great, and she's had a hard life. Just... be nice."

"Don't worry, buddy. It's just one date." But he admitted—though only to himself—that Livy was the first woman who'd grabbed his attention in a long time. A very long time. His business kept him so busy. But it appeared Livy's work kept her just as busy.

Well, it would do them both good to take a night off.

EMILY SLAMMED through the front door of their house. "Mom, I'm home."

"In the kitchen."

Emily hurried into the room. "Oh, hey. Guess what. Delbert is probably going to hire Austin to do some work for Cabot Hotel. And maybe the whole Hamilton Hotel chain." Emily snagged an apple from the bowl on the counter and crunched a bite. "And Delbert is going to let me work on doing the updates for social media for the hotel. How cool is that?"

"Very cool." She was proud of all the challenges Emily had taken on this year. And she had to admit the idea of Austin being around more didn't sound so bad either.

"Austin said he'd train me and help make up a content calendar. I'm going to learn so much from him." Emily's face flushed with excitement.

"Sounds like it." Livy hung up the dishtowel she'd been using to dry the dishes. "Oh, there's a package for you over there on the counter. From your dad."

Emily moved over to the end of the counter and eyed the package. "Wonder what it is? It's not my birthday or anything."

"Why don't you open it and find out?"

Emily tore open the package and gasped as she opened it. "Wow, Mom, look at this." She held up a new cell phone. "This is the newest model they have. So cool."

Everything was *cool* with Emily these days.

Emily opened a card that was with the package and read it out loud. "Em, thought you might like this. I'm pretty hit and miss on your birthday but wanted you to have this. It's all set up and the bill will come to me. Enjoy."

"That's a very nice gift." Something she'd never be able to give Emily. New model cell phones were way out of her budget.

Emily opened the box and pulled out the shiny new phone. "This is like the best gift ever."

Ouch.

"You should call your father and thank him."

"I will. And I'll go change before we head over to Grams." Emily hurried out of the room.

Livy sank onto a chair at the kitchen table. It *was* a nice gift. Very nice. And she liked Emily to have nice things. Her daughter would love the phone. It was nice of Brett to send it.

Nice, nice, nice.

So... why was she so upset? She sighed and stood back up. She'd go change, too. Maybe they'd take the boat over to her mom's house for dinner. Fresh air on the ride would do her good. Help her get over her ridiculous... jealousy? That Brett could afford to buy Emily gifts like the phone for no occasion, just because.

Drop it and go get dressed.

CHAPTER 8

The next evening Olivia texted Emily that she was headed to Jimmy's for dinner. Emily would assume it was with Heather. No need to go into details. Emily was out with friends tonight, so she had the house to herself to get ready in.

She stared into the depths of her closet. She didn't spend much on herself for things like nice clothes, but certainly, she must have something to wear that didn't look like it had been in her closet for years—which it probably had.

She finally found a simple red sundress. That would work. She slipped on red sandals and looked in the mirror. Her curly hair danced wildly around her shoulders, as usual. She took a silver clip and swept her hair up, capturing the curls. There, that was better.

She headed to Jimmy's with time to spare, wanting to be sure she wasn't late. When she got to the restaurant, Austin was already waiting for her. He waved when he saw her come in.

He stood as she approached the table and pulled out a worn wooden barstool for her. "Hi." His eyes sparkled with appreciation. "You look nice."

"Ah... thanks." She sat down, suddenly nervous.

He sat across from her. "I've been looking at the menu. I want like everything on it."

She laughed at that understatement. "It's all very good here."

"And right here on the bay. The view is great. And the beer is cold." He pointed to his glass. "I got here a bit early—didn't want to keep you waiting—so I went ahead and ordered a drink."

So he hadn't wanted to keep her waiting, either. *Was he as nervous as she was feeling now?*

If so, there certainly was no sign of it in his sky-blue eyes.

The server came over. "Hey, Livy. Usual beer?"

"Yes, please."

"So you have a usual beer here? And of course, they know you." His mouth curved into an amused grin.

"I come here with Heather quite a bit when she's in town. And I do have a favorite beer. A local craft beer."

"I'll try that next."

They ordered their meals, then sat and sipped their drinks, enjoying the view and the soft music coming from the lone guitar player at the far end of the deck. She slowly began to relax as they chatted.

See, this wasn't so bad.

She looked over at him, watching him enjoying his meal. The light breeze barely ruffled his short brown hair. His blue knit shirt pulled across his broad shoulders. A relaxed expression settled on his features across his strong jawline. He looked up and caught her staring at him, and she ducked her head.

"Moonbeam is quite the hidden gem," Austin said nonchalantly as if he hadn't just caught her staring. "Jesse always talked about how great it was, but I had no idea. The town is charming. A bit of an old-fashioned small-town feeling."

Talk about the town. That was a safe, easy subject. "I love it here. Though, honestly, I've never lived anywhere else. Well, except for a couple of years of college. Then I moved back because—" She shrugged. "Emily." And suddenly the easy conversation became personal.

AUSTIN DIDN'T KNOW if he should ask questions or press her regarding Emily, so he hid behind another sip of his beer—the last sip. He raised his hand to the server and motioned that he'd have the same beer that Livy had ordered.

He'd caught her staring at him, and he wondered what she thought after her perusal. Luckily she hadn't caught him when he'd been staring at her while she searched the menu, though she said she had it memorized.

Livy continued. "I dropped out of school and I moved back to Moonbeam and in with Mom. It just seemed to make sense. Mom helped me a lot."

He wanted to ask if she'd ever gone back to school, but once again, he was uncertain about posing the question.

"I'm just now finally finishing up my degree."

Was she reading his thoughts?

"Really?"

"Yes, in business."

"Well, that should come in handy with Parker's and the cafe."

"It sure has so far. I should be finished up soon and finally have that degree in my hand."

He looked over at this hard-working woman. A businesswoman, a mother, and a student. He was a bit in awe of her and all that she juggled.

She seemed oblivious of his admiration as she promptly changed the subject. "So, how about you? Did you speak to Delbert yet? Emily said that he was thinking of hiring you to overhaul their online presence."

"I did talk to him and he hired. Looks like I'm going to stick around Moonbeam for a bit. I can work from anywhere, so that's no problem. I'd like to be here to get The Cabot all set up and train Emily on how to post things, what to post, and help make a social media calendar. Plus, I'm still working on Jesse's site." He took a breath and plunged on. "And... if you like... I want to work on yours too."

"Sounds like you're busy with paying jobs

KAY CORRELL

and I... I don't think I can swing any more expenses right now. Even if online ordering would be great."

He frowned. "We could work something out. I'm sure we could."

"I can't ask that of you."

He grinned, hoping to win her over. "You didn't ask. I offered."

"No, I just... can't."

He was going to have to find a different way to approach this. He could see the pride in her eyes. She didn't want to accept help. Even if he wanted so badly to give it to her. And he wasn't sure why he wanted to help her out so much. Jesse was probably right—he was just a lifelong helper person. It was just who he was. If his knowledge could benefit someone else, he loved to lend a hand.

Okay, he did like his paying gigs, too. They paid for his nice condo in Denver and all his techie toys like the newest computer and latest model phone. But that didn't mean he couldn't make time to help Livy. He'd just have to figure out a way...

"Well, I'm here to help if you want me to."

"Thanks." She smiled, but the expression didn't leave much hope that she'd accept his aid.

He decided to change the subject. "So, Delbert threw in a sweetener to hiring me. A room at The Cabot for while I'm in town."

Her eyes lit up. "Really? That's wonderful. I love how it turned out."

"Evidently he has a two-bedroom suite that some of the furniture for the second bedroom had to be returned and he's waiting on delivery. So, he's letting me stay there in the bedroom that is furnished. It has a small kitchenette, and the main room has a nice large desk. I'm going to move over there tomorrow."

"What did Jesse say about that?"

"He offered to let me stay with him as long as I wanted, but I know it's hard. He's lived alone forever, and I'm always underfoot. This will work out better."

Their dinner was delivered, and they ate and chatted. It was fun getting to know her better, and she asked him a million questions.

"So, where are you from?" she asked.

"I live in Denver. Well, out of Denver a bit. Just on the mountain side. Grew up in Michigan, though. Ended up in Denver for a job, then stayed there when I opened my own business. It's close to the mountains and I love to go hiking."

"I've never been to Colorado. The photos of it look beautiful, though."

"It really is a beautiful part of the country. I love living there. Though, I'm out of town quite a bit for business when I get new big jobs. I always like to go to the client's main office to get a feel for the business."

"How did you get into this whole social media business?" She dipped her hushpuppy into some melted butter, popped it into her mouth, and grinned as she wiped her hand across her mouth. "I love the hushpuppies here."

"They are good," he agreed. "And I got into the social media aspect at my second job in Denver. Social media was growing, and the company was young and hungry. The owner was intent on using all aspects of social media and their website. I learned a lot from him. Sharp guy. But the company was bought out by this big conglomerate, and they let go about half the people. I was one of the ones let go."

"I'm sorry."

"No, it was a blessing in disguise. I was worried at first. Bills to pay and everything. I was stupid, and I'd been spending everything I earned. But I decided there was no time like the present to start up my own company." He grinned sheepishly. "I know it was crazy. But I was lucky enough to get a large client right off the bat from a recommendation of someone I'd worked with before. I started saving my money after that. Didn't ever want to be out of a job with no savings again."

"I hear you on wanting to have some safety savings in the bank. It was a couple of years after I had Emily before I could start saving. And that was with living at Mom's. Finally saved up some, and Emily and I moved out to our own place. Though Mom helped with the down payment on that. I've paid her back now." She paused and took a sip of her drink.

He tried not to stare at her while she talked. Like the way her curls had escaped the silver clip in her hair, or the neutral shade of polish on her nails, or the fact her lipstick had worn off her lips and a bit of it clung to her beer glass.

Oblivious to his thoughts, she continued. "And I still keep adding to savings every paycheck I can. I've got to save for Emily's college, too, though she's hoping for some scholarships. She's really smart and the top of her class. I'm hoping she gets scholarship money, too. That would really help. Though she's worked hard and saved up all her work money toward college."

"She seems like a really great kid."

"She is... she's... well, she's the best. I'm lucky to be her mom."

He wanted to ask about Emily's father but didn't. He looked across the table, half expecting Livy to say something about him. She just dunked another hushpuppy in the melted butter. The mind-reading connection must be broken.

They finished their meal and strolled along the wharf under the canopy of twinkling white lights and music spilling out from a music group in a large open area. He couldn't remember the last time he'd had such an enjoyable evening. She glanced up at him and smiled. His pulse quickened at the sight of her smile. He glanced down at her hand and wondered if he could take it in his. Too soon? Should he even be starting anything with her?

Jesse's voice played over and over in his mind. *Don't mess with her. Just be... nice.*

"Look at you two." The Jenkins twins hurried up to them in purposeful strides.

"Hello, ladies." He wasn't sure which was which or who was who.

"I thought you two weren't dating?" Twin One said.

He was fully willing to tell the ladies they *were* dating, but he looked at Livy, wondering how she'd answer.

"We... we just had dinner at Jimmy's."

"Out to dinner qualifies as a date in my book," Twin Two said.

"I agree with you one hundred percent." He nodded soberly and turned to Livy. "So, I guess we should officially call this our first date. There's no avoiding it."

She quirked an eyebrow in surprise. "Really?"

"There you have it. Your first date." Twin One... or was it Two... said.

"But we should go now. Nice seeing you two." Livy tilted her head toward the long walkway.

He nodded. "Yes, we must run. Nice seeing you two ladies again." He took Livy's arm and her eyes widened.

They took a few steps, and she whispered, "What are you doing? You're just feeding the gossip frenzy."

"Ah, a little town gossip won't hurt anything.

They looked so pleased to be able to break the next big tidbit."

She laughed. "You have no idea what you've started."

No, he didn't really have a clear idea of what he'd started. But he sure wanted to find out.

CHAPTER 9

O livia walked arm in arm with Austin, with just one quick glance back at Jackie and Jillian. They were still watching, their heads close together, intent on talking to each other. Probably charting out the best way to spread the gossip.

Austin paused when they got to the beginning of the wharf. "So... can I walk you home?"

She considered her options. She didn't mind walking home alone. She walked around alone at night all the time in Moonbeam. But she wouldn't mind having the company, either. She glanced at her watch. She probably still had time before Emily came home.

"Uh... sure." *How was that for some resounding*

enthusiasm for his offer? She smiled to soften her weak response. Hopefully, Emily would still be out with her friends. Not that she cared if Emily knew she went to dinner with Austin, but she just wasn't ready for the questions that were sure to be fired at her.

He shortened his stride to match hers as they slowly strolled toward her home, walking in and out of the lamplight. The night favored them with perfect weather with stars peeking out from the few clouds that drifted high above them.

"You know, you're just going to have to walk all the way back across town to Jesse's cottage." She paused at a crossroad that would take Austin to Jesse's. "This road is a shortcut to his house. I can make it home fine from here."

"Nah, I don't mind the extra walk to your house. It's a nice night out." He grinned and patted his stomach. "The exercise will do me good. I've been dining out on the town's excellent cuisine ever since I got here."

He could pat his stomach all he wanted, but it looked rock hard beneath his shirt… Not that she'd noticed.

They continued down the road toward her home. When they got there, they climbed the front steps and stood with the low glow from her front porch light pouring over them, making a warm, inviting circle around them. "I had a nice time tonight." She smiled at him. It had been a fun, relaxing evening.

"I did too. I was wondering... would you like to do it again? I mean go out again?" He gave her a conspiratorial wink. "You know, now that we know tonight was an official date. At least according to the Jenkins twins."

She didn't have a chance to answer—which was good because she didn't know what she wanted to answer—because they were interrupted when a car pulled into the drive and Emily got out, waving bye to her friends as she approached.

"See, made curfew with minutes to spare." Emily looked from her to Austin and back to her, with questioning eyes.

She glanced at her watch. "You sure did."

"Hi, Austin." Emily stood on the steps, the quizzical look still firmly in place.

"Hi, there." Austin took a tiny step back.

"Austin and I... we had dinner at Jimmy's."

Emily raised an eyebrow. "Oh. Did you run into each other there?"

"Ah, no. We made plans to meet."

"Like a date?" Emily asked plainly.

"Em, why don't you go on in? I'll be inside in a minute."

Emily gave her a long, hard stare. "Sure. Night, Austin." Emily slipped inside the house. Bright light spilled out onto the porch as she switched on the lights inside.

It broke the intimate circle of warm light that had surrounded them. Broke the spell. The coziness that had encircled them.

She took a step back, sharply feeling the distance between them now. "I should go in."

"I take it she didn't know we had a date." He tilted his head.

She couldn't tell if she saw hurt or confusion or just questioning in his eyes.

"No, I hadn't mentioned it to her." Or to anyone. She looked down at her pretty red sandals for a moment, noticing she could really do with a new pedicure. She finally looked back up and found him staring directly at her, waiting. She shrugged. "It's difficult for me. I'm always trying to protect her. I don't like to bring people into her life... and have them leave."

"And I'm just here for a bit while I work." He nodded. "Maybe it's best if we don't try the dating thing. I understand. You have to think of Emily first."

"And I'm really busy at the cafe." The excuse sounded lame, even to her.

"Okay, well, I'll probably see you around." He turned and climbed down the stairs, then swiveled back and gave her a small smile. "I did have a good time tonight." Then he disappeared down the street as she stood watching.

A strange feeling of regret filtered through her. Had she been ready to say yes to going on a second date with him? They'd never know now, would they?

She sighed and went into the house, bracing herself to face a million questions from her daughter.

And Emily did not disappoint.

CHAPTER 10

Donna entered Sea Glass Cafe. Olivia had finally settled on that name for certain—it was painted on the front window. She liked the name her daughter had picked. It was cute and beachy and fit the coastal decor Olivia had found for the cafe. She'd even given up some of her glass jars of sea glass and placed them on shelves around the room. Cute wooden signs saying things like *this way to the beach* or *flip-flop zone* adorned the walls.

She hurried through the main room of the cafe and found her sister busy stocking the cabinets.

Evelyn turned and smiled at her, though a look of exhaustion hovered in her eyes. "Most of the supplies are in." She pointed to a checklist resting on the counter. "We should be all ready to open on the date Olivia picked. Two weeks from now."

"That's great." She wasn't sure if the exhaustion in Evelyn's eyes was from working so hard to get the cafe ready or more stress from her impending divorce. Either way, she was worried about her sister.

Evelyn picked up the checklist and glanced at it. "I'm getting ready to do some test baking. Want to be sure I know how this oven heats. Commercial ovens are so different than my own. Anyway, I'll bring the food home tonight for dinner."

"That's one great thing about having you live with me for a bit. You're always cooking and you're a way better chef than I am." Donna grinned. "Although I'm going to pack on the pounds if you don't quit with all the sweets."

"I'm just going through all of great-grandmother's recipes. Trying to figure out which ones to use. I've decided I'm going to rotate through them. Different things every day. Hoping that will keep people coming back to try different items. Then, I'll probably settle on a few that we have available all the time."

"I hope you decide to keep Grace Parker's peach pie as a regular. I do love that."

"I know that's your favorite. Has been since we were little girls."

"Looks like you and Olivia have this whole cafe thing under control." Though she was worried about it. Not that she'd say anything to Olivia. She hoped the cafe could bring a profit to Parker's because they really couldn't afford to keep it open if it didn't. And then what would they do with all the expanded space? They'd have to sell it and try to squeeze their inventory back into the original Parker's space, a task she dreaded to think of now that they'd moved so much over and connected the two buildings. The main Parker building was now looking like a cute, old-fashioned general store instead of the packed-in-every-single-inch shop it had become before the expansion.

"Olivia is a smart businesswoman. Wish I'd been that smart at her age." Evelyn frowned. "Then maybe I wouldn't be in this whole divorce mess without any money."

"Your lawyer still hasn't found a way for you to get anything?" Donna frowned.

"Not with that prenuptial I signed in my

silly, naive youth." Evelyn shook her head. "And Darren is pushing for a quick divorce."

"I'm so sorry, Evie."

Evelyn shrugged and turned to continue loading the shelves. "I'm getting used to the idea that I'm soon going to be a divorced woman. And I was lucky to find this job at the cafe with Olivia. It's not like I've worked any jobs. I was just Darren's wife and threw business dinners and ran charity events."

"You did a great job with the grand opening of The Cabot."

"Oh, that reminds me. Guess what? Delbert wants to hold a big Christmas party there and he's hired me to plan and run that, too. He pays... really well. I'm hoping with working here at the cafe and taking on some more event planning jobs that I'll soon be able to save up enough to move out."

"There's absolutely no hurry on you moving out," Donna insisted. She actually liked having someone living in the house with her again.

"But I want to move out. Not that I don't like living with you," Evelyn hurried to explain. "But I've never once lived on my own... and now it's become this big goal of mine. Find my own place. Live alone."

"Then I'm sure you'll make it happen."

"There you two are."

Donna and Evelyn whirled around in unison at the sound of their mother's voice.

"Mother, what are you doing here?" Donna couldn't remember the last time her mother had walked through the doors of Parker's.

"I came to see what all this brouhaha about a cafe inside of Parker's was all about." She glanced around at the disarray in the kitchen. "Really, Donna, why are you doing this? It makes no sense. Not to mention, the days of a general store are long past. Don't you think it's time to move on? I bet you could get good money for selling Parker's. It's in a great location." Their mother's disapproval was clear. But then Patricia Beale never was one to keep her opinions to herself.

"I think the cafe was a wonderful idea." Evelyn jumped in to support Donna's decision.

She sent her sister a grateful look, but gutsy move on her sister's part. It didn't usually go well to contradict their mother.

"Mother, I have absolutely no plans of selling Parker's. Ever. It's been in the family for generations. Why would we sell it?"

"Because the property is worth so much

now?" Her mother picked up a bag of sugar from the counter and frowned at it like it was some kind of foreign object before setting it back down.

"And you." Her mother turned to look directly at Evelyn. "Have you squashed this silly divorce nonsense? Made up with Darren for whatever you did that annoyed him into this ridiculous request for a divorce?"

Evelyn squared her shoulders. "Mother, I didn't do anything. Darren just decided to move on with someone new. Someone younger. Whatever. He's the one wanting the divorce."

"But have you talked to him? Surely you can convince him how silly the idea of a divorce is. We Beales don't get divorced."

Their mother apparently had forgotten about Donna's long-ago divorce. Or, more likely, was just ignoring it.

"What will people at the Country Club say?" Their mother shook her head, her mouth curved with a look of censure.

"I wouldn't know, Mother. Darren has taken me off our membership and none of the ladies there have spoken to me in months."

"I just don't know how you let this happen."

Donna decided it was time to step in.

"Mother, Evelyn didn't *let* this happen. She's been a wonderful wife to Darren. He's just... a self-centered jerk, and now he wants some young girl on his arm. Good riddance."

"Donna, don't talk like that. Darren is a good man. So successful. Maybe he'll come to his senses. We can only hope."

Ah, Darren made good money, the one yardstick her mother used to judge all people and all things.

Evelyn's eyes flashed with determination. "Mother, I don't hope that. I wouldn't take him back if he asked—which he's not going to. I don't trust him, and I'll never put myself in a position where a man can hurt me like that again."

"All men have their little side affairs. It's what they do. You need to just wait him out. Don't sign any papers. He can't get a divorce without you signing off on it, now can he? Just stall until he gets over this little thing he's going through." Patricia Beale was never one to let someone dissuade her when she was certain she was correct.

"Mother, let's change the subject, shall we?" Donna interrupted. "How are things at the retirement village?"

"The idiots who run it are not keeping it up

to the standards that were promised when your father and I moved there." The corners of her mouth turned down in a disapproving frown. "I'm not certain what I'll do. Some of my friends there are moving to a new retirement community." She sighed. "But I hate to think of the work involved with moving."

Like her mother had lifted a single finger when she and their father moved from Moonbeam to the retirement place in Naples?

"I'm sure you'll find a new place if you're not happy where you are," Donna said.

"I resent the fact that I even have to look around again. It was draining when your father and I looked the first time."

If Donna remembered correctly, her father carefully combed through all the retirement areas in Southwest Florida and specifically picked this one for its reputation and the number of *important* people he knew of that had moved there. Her mother had been presented with a done deal. Not that it mattered. Her mom always went along with whatever her father commanded.

"They are just finishing up that new retirement community in Moonbeam. I heard it's really nice," Evelyn said.

What? Was her sister crazy? Did she really want their mother to move back to town and bring all this negativity and disapproval for their every decision back here on a daily basis? She shot Evelyn an incredulous look.

"Though, I doubt that it would be nice enough. And it would be difficult to move back to such a small town after living in Naples. Naples has such great amenities. And culture. And... well... Moonbeam has none of that." Her mother shook her head. "It doesn't even have any nice places to have a meal."

Okay, then. The cafe was just going to serve crummy food. Good to know. "You're probably right, Mother. You'd be happier in Naples." Donna nodded in agreement to her mother's love of Naples.

"Yes, definitely." Her mother glanced around the cafe. "I still think this was a foolish move on your part, Donna. Mark my words. But I must run. I need to get back home for an afternoon tea with some of the ladies. We're going to discuss options and whether we're all going to move out or try and get the retirement village administration to step up and do their jobs correctly."

"Well, good luck." Donna walked her

mother out of the kitchen and to the front door. "Drive safely."

"Oh, I had a driver bring me today. I'm not driving much these days." And with that surprising comment, her mother walked out the door. When had that started? Her mother had driven over after she returned from her world cruise. Wasn't that just a few weeks ago? She shrugged. Maybe she liked being driven around. Her father used to do most of the driving.

Donna headed back to the kitchen and found her sister sitting in a chair. "Hey, Evie, don't listen to her. She just... spouts her opinions."

"I know. It's just... wow. She reminded me of how I never lived up to Darren's expectations, either. He was always telling me I'd done this or that wrong."

"Good, then it helps to make you remember how great it is to get him out of your life." She cocked her head to one side. "But what were you thinking telling mother about the new retirement community here in town? Are you crazy? Can you imagine having Mom and her opinions here all the time?"

Evelyn gave her a weak smile. "No, I guess I

can't. It just seems wrong to want your own mother to be over an hour away, though."

"No, I think it's *sane* to want that." She grinned. "Very sane."

CHAPTER 11

Austin sat at a large table in the library room of The Cabot Hotel. Emily sat beside him, eagerly peering at the computer. She'd been a quick study on all he'd taught her the last week or so. She'd watched everything he'd done. While he updated the website and opened social media accounts, she asked a continual stream of questions. He didn't mind though. She was an eager student. He was certain she'd be able to handle posting to the social media accounts for the hotel.

"I can't believe all you taught me," Emily said. "I thought I knew a lot of this stuff. I've taken every techie class my high school offers. That and history. I love both. But I've learned so much from you."

"You're a quick learner."

"Thanks."

"Say, how would you like to learn how to install some software programs on websites? Like maybe an online ordering system?"

"Really?" Her eyes lit up. "That would be awesome."

"We could add one for the Sea Glass Cafe if you get your mother's okay. I'd love to show you how to install it and set up the ordering."

"Wow, that would be great. I'm going to know so much of this stuff. Maybe I can get some side jobs doing this techie work to help pay for college."

"I bet you can. It's a good skill set to learn. And I could give you a list of some good online classes that are available to help you learn. Maybe your high school could coordinate getting credit for them? Or even advanced college credits?"

"That would be fantastic." Emily jumped up. "I'm going to go talk to Mom right now. I'm sure she'll say yes. I really want to learn this. Thanks, Austin."

Emily hurried away, and he sat back. A small smile tugged at his lips at his hopefully brilliant solution to helping out Livy. Maybe, just maybe, she'd accept help this way. She'd want Emily to learn the new skills, wouldn't she?

AUSTIN CLEARED up his work at his desk in his room. It was almost time for dinner and his stomach growled, reminding him how famished he was. He still held a self-satisfied feeling about suggesting Emily learn the ordering software.

A loud knock at the door echoed through the room. He crossed over and opened it, surprised to see Livy standing there, fire in her stormy blue eyes.

"Uh... come in?" He took a step back.

She strode into the room and whirled around to face him. "So... that's how you work? You suggest you'll teach my daughter something since I wouldn't let you do that work for free? I told you that we just don't have the money now for this online system and getting it installed and running. I don't want your charity."

"It's not charity. I enjoy working with Emily. And I get the software at a discount. It's reasonably priced. I thought Emily would like to learn a new skill. She's a quick learner and I enjoy teaching her."

"She came to the store with all these big plans and chattering about getting advanced college credit and... well... I'm not made of money. Things are tight. How am I going to get funds to keep the cafe running until it turns a profit and pay for college credits for Emily at the same time?" She sank onto a chair. "I'm just trying to survive. And do the best I can for my daughter."

"Of course you are." He sat in the chair across from her. "I didn't mean to cause problems, and I should have spoken with you first. But I truly don't mind showing her how to install the package. It isn't hard. And she can then set up the items you want for online ordering. She'll learn a new skill and you'll have an ordering system."

She stared at him for a moment. Stared hard. He could see the exact moment she started to waver.

"I am sorry, Livy. I didn't mean to overstep."

"I guess that's not the worst idea I've ever heard." She gave him a weak grin.

He gave her a wide one in return. "I thought it was actually a brilliant idea. Everyone gets what they want."

Her mouth quirked up at one corner. "I

admit, I'm not one for accepting help. I like to do things on my own."

"Really? I hadn't noticed." He sent her a fake incredulous look.

"Honestly, though. Thank you. I do appreciate this. Not only because it will help the cafe, but because Emily is so excited about everything you've been showing her."

"I've enjoyed it. Honest." He looked over at her. "So... you could repay me, though..."

"How's that?"

"I'm starving and I'm tired of eating alone. Want to go grab something to eat? Doesn't have to be a date. I know you don't want that. But just dinner with a friend who is starving to death?"

Her eyes brimmed with amusement. "I could do that. Just to save him from certain death."

"Perfect. Pick the place."

"I haven't had a chance to eat here in the dining room of The Cabot. Or are you tired of dining here since you've been here a few days?"

"No, that sounds great. Closer to the food." He gave her another grin. "Let's go."

"Okay, just let me text Emily. She's at a

study group tonight but I'll let her know it will be a bit before I'm home."

She texted a message, then slipped the phone back into her pocket. "All set."

They left his room and headed down to the dining room. All in all, he was pretty pleased with how his day was turning out.

CHAPTER 12

Olivia couldn't figure out how she'd gone to see Austin so furious with his end-run at getting the website ordering system set up to having dinner with him now. She looked down at her navy skirt and Parker's t-shirt and wished she'd worn something nicer. But how was she supposed to know when she'd come over to The Cabot to give Austin a piece of her mind that she'd end up having dinner in their fancy dining room?

And while things were confusing her, why had she blurted out her financial worries to him? She always kept them to herself. Didn't even really talk about them to Heather. And here she'd just dumped it all out in the open for

Austin to see. She chastised herself the whole time they walked to the dining room.

They got a table by the window overlooking the bay and both ordered a glass of wine. The server brought them menus, and she grimaced at the prices. Higher than she'd expected. But really, he was doing so much for her, and she was determined to snag the bill.

They ordered their meals—she found the least expensive item on the menu for herself —and sat and sipped their wine.

"So, Emily... she's really smart. A quick learner. But I'm sure you know that." Austin sat back and stretched out his long legs. They brushed hers under the table, but he didn't seem to notice.

She noticed but ignored it. "Emily is smart. I'm so proud of her. She does well in school and works hard at her jobs. She's starting to look at colleges."

"She says she's interested in history and technology. That's quite a combination."

Olivia grinned. "It is. But she's passionate about both of them. I'm pretty sure technology will support her better, but I just want her to find a job she loves."

"Do you love working at Parker's?" Austin asked.

That was a hard question to answer. She paused while she chose her words. "I—well, I never really considered anything different. Mom was helping me raise Emily and needed help at the store. Plus, I grew up working there part-time. It just made sense to keep working there."

"Do you ever dream of doing something else?" He watched her intently.

Too intently. She tried not to squirm under his gaze. He asked tough questions. "I used to. A bit. But then we built the cafe, and it's all mine to run and make decisions on. That helps. I feel like it's something of my own that I'm creating, I'm making happen." She looked down at her silverware and straightened it before looking back up at him. "But I really don't want to let my mom down. I need for the cafe to be a success. To contribute to our income."

"I have no doubt you'll make it a success."

"I like your enthusiasm, but we won't really know until it's up and running."

"The online ordering should help, don't you think? Sometimes people just want to pick up a quick meal and take it back to work or home for dinner."

"If you're trying to get me to say that the online system is a great idea... it is. I just worry that we're doing too much, too quickly."

"We could get it set up and get Emily used to how it works but not bring it live until you have time to settle into running things."

"That's probably a good idea. Maybe wait a month or so." She thought about it. At least that would be one less thing she'd have to juggle while she handled any opening glitches.

"So, I hear you picked a grand opening date. Emily was already working on some graphics for it to post to your TalkTime page."

"Yes, it's next Friday. I'm excited and... a bit scared." To be honest, she was a lot scared, but she didn't tell him that. "We're planning on having baked goods and great coffee for breakfast. I swear I've tasted at least a billion brands and types of coffee."

"Great coffee is important." He gave her his affable smile. The one that assured her he was truly listening to her. Enjoying her company. Enjoying the conversation.

"Then we'll have sandwiches and soups for lunch and supper. We'll see how that goes at first, then might expand the menu. Evelyn is an excellent baker. She'll do the baking and make the bread for the sandwiches. We'll get the malt machine up and running again and still serve our ice cream."

"Jesse assures me you have the best ice cream on the planet." Austin's eyes brightened. "I love ice cream."

"I will admit it's good. It's Grace Parker's recipe. Or maybe her daughter, Mary Lou's. We're not really sure. But my great-grandmother, Mary Lou, opened up the malt counter at Parker's."

"I can't wait to try it."

"We'll have some ice cream the beginning of next week. You should come by and try some. On the house, of course."

"I'll do that."

Their meals were delivered, and they continued their casual conversation. She liked that he was so easy to talk to. "So, are you enjoying staying at The Cabot?"

"I am. Though I will admit to missing the long beach walks I took every morning at Jesse's house. It was nice to have the beach just right out the door."

"I bet it is nice to live on the beach."

"But you're right on the waterway."

"We are, and I love having the boat right out

the door to go for boat rides. We often take it over to Mom's. It's faster than driving over."

"I pulled up a map of the town the other day. The canal system is fascinating. You can wind your way from the harbor or the coastal waterway or out to the gulf. There's that peninsula Jesse lives on that's lined with cottages right on the gulf. It's like the town has a little bit of everything."

"It does. I love living here."

"I bet. And you have your family here. That's nice."

"Where's your family?"

His lips spread into a wide grin. "Ah, my family. They are spread all over, but we always head home for Christmas."

"Where is home?"

"Home is in Michigan. Moved there when I was a kid. We're all planning on heading back there for Christmas, and I'm trying to schedule a trip at the end of the summer. My mother... she hasn't been doing that well. Cancer. But she's a fighter and determined to beat it." He glanced away, then back at her. "I'm sure she will."

"I'm really sorry, Austin." She reached out and covered his hand with hers.

He looked down at her hand, then back up into her eyes. "She'll beat it." He reasserted his conviction. "And they are great parents. Went to every sports game I ever played in. Every event at school." He paused, then continued. "I'm lucky to have them."

She realized she was still holding his hand and slowly took her hand back and settled it in her lap.

"How about you? I know you have Emily, and your Mom, and Heather and your aunt. Any more family here?"

"My grandmother lives in Naples at a retirement place."

"That must be nice."

"It's... complicated. I love her, I do. She's just very critical of most everything. She's a hard woman to... well, to be around. And my grandfather was the hardest, most critical, most judgmental man ever born. They mostly left my mom and Evelyn with my great-grandparents. My grandparents traveled a lot, and I wasn't ever certain why they had kids. They weren't involved in mom and Aunt Evelyn's lives very much. Always off somewhere for business or pleasure. But Mom and Aunt Evelyn loved living with their grandparents. She said they had the best times there. So I guess it all worked out."

"Some people just aren't cut out to be parents, I guess."

"I guess not. Like my own father."

Austin didn't ask, but his eyebrow did raise up questioningly.

"He left my mom when I was young. I rarely see him. And he's seen Emily once when she was a young girl, just a toddler really."

"I'm sorry."

"Don't be. Like you said. Some people just aren't meant to be parents. I lucked out in the Mom department though. Mom is great. I don't know what I would have done without her when I got pregnant with Emily. She let me move home and helped with... everything, really."

She could see the questions brewing in his eyes and decided that now was as good a time as any to explain about Emily's dad.

"And I guess you're wondering about Em's dad."

"I admit to being a bit curious." He nodded.

"We never married. We were so not ready for that. We weren't right for each other, either. Not for something permanent. He moved away, finished college up East. He calls Em occasionally. Sends presents now and then." Like the stupidly expensive cell phone for no reason. "And he visits her sometimes. Hasn't been here in over a year, though."

"She's good with that?"

"She understands it. Not an ideal parental situation, but she's had Mom around her whole life, too. And Evelyn. And Heather. Anyway, we've all adapted to how it all turned out."

She spied the server heading toward the table and got ready to snatch the bill when he put it down, a bit worried to see the total, but determined it was hers to pay. She glanced up as the server got closer.

"Mr. Hamilton said tonight's dinner was on him," the server said.

She didn't know whether to feel relief at avoiding the pricey meal ticket or bothered that she hadn't been able to pay Austin back for all his help. "Tell him thank you. That was really nice."

"Yes, give him my thanks, too," Austin chimed in as he stood and came around the table to pull her chair out and help her to her feet.

Austin walked by Livy's side out to the lobby of The Cabot. People were milling around and gathered in groups at the many clusters of seating scattered around. Fresh flowers adorned the tables spread throughout the area, and dancing light shone down from the opulent chandelier. The lobby never ceased to awe him slightly when he entered it.

They headed to the front door. "I'd like to walk you home."

"You don't have to do that."

"I could use the exercise..." He gave her a small smile. "And I'm not ready for the night to end."

He wasn't ready. He loved talking to her and had been strangely pleased—for his sake—that Emily's dad was out of the picture. Though, that was a rather selfish thought since Emily would probably love for him to be around more.

Livy paused in the doorway. "Okay, if you'd like the walk..."

Perfect. He led the way outside. The skies were just beginning to darken and a few stars twinkled above them. They walked down the long circular drive out to the street. She turned to the left, and he laughed. "I keep thinking I'm getting to know my way around Moonbeam, but I'd swear we'd go right out of here."

"You can actually go either way. This way we avoid the main street—Magnolia Avenue —and take some side streets to my house. I thought you might like taking a different route."

"Sounds like a plan." He shortened his strides to match hers and they headed down the sidewalk.

She pointed out the church that her great-grandparents, grandparents, and parents had been married in and the small graveyard beside it where so many generations in her family were buried. They passed a small park with a charming gazebo lit up with white Christmas lights.

"They keep the lights up all year long," she explained.

They finally turned onto her street and reached her house. A fact that he was sorry for. He still wasn't ready for the night to end. She unlocked the door but stood on the porch with the warm glow highlighting her hair, and she looked... beautiful.

Jesse's words reverberated through his mind. *Don't mess with her. Just... be nice.*

He put all thoughts of kissing those lips of hers firmly away. Kinda.

"You know how to get back to The Cabot? The direct route is just taking my street, turn right at the end, and it will eventually wind up on Magnolia. Then you can find your way to Harborside, right?"

"Yes, I'm good."

"Good night. And thank you for all you're doing for Emily. And for Parker's and the cafe." Her eyes radiated warmth and gratitude. Not that he noticed. "I should go in."

And though he wanted to reach out and take her hand and ask her to stay outside with him for just a bit longer, he didn't. With one last smile, she slipped inside. He turned and climbed down the stairs and headed back to The Cabot. Loneliness—a very unfamiliar feeling—settled over him.

CHAPTER 13

Donna watched as Melody Tanner walked into Parker's and grabbed a few items from the shelves, then came to check out.

"Hi, Melody. How are you?"

"I'm... fine." Melody gave her a small smile. "Could I put this on my account?"

Melody's balance was growing each week, but Donna didn't have the heart to say no to the new, young widow. "Of course." She rang up the items.

"Thanks, Donna."

"Say, you don't happen to know someone who wants a part-time job, do you? We need some extra help here at Parker's with the expanded store and opening the cafe."

Melody's eyes brightened. "Oh, I haven't worked in years, but I did use to be a waitress, so I have experience. And... I could really use a job."

"Really? That would be wonderful." Donna bobbed her head enthusiastically. "Let me talk to Olivia. I bet we can work something out."

"I'd love that." Melody scribbled her phone number on a piece of paper and set it on the counter when she picked up the bag with her order.

"I'll call you soon." Donna smiled at the woman, hoping they could make this work out for her. She hated to think that Melody was getting in over her head in debt. Besides, she was a charming woman and would be a good asset for Parker's.

"Thank you so much. This would just be... perfect."

Melody left the store, and Donna looked at the slip of paper in her hand. They *could* use more help. She just hoped that Olivia wouldn't mind that she offered up waitressing. She was well aware that Olivia wanted the cafe to be all hers. Donna left Lydia in charge of the checkout and went to find her daughter.

Olivia was arranging the tables and chairs around in the cafe. "Hi, Mom."

"Hi. Listen... I might have overstepped, but it just kind of happened."

Olivia paused and looked at her. "What happened?"

"So, Melody Tanner was just in."

"Did she ask for more credit?"

"She did... and I suggested we could use her help here at Parker's."

"I didn't know you wanted to hire someone else."

"I thought with the cafe opening that we could use someone to help wait tables or help out in the kitchen? I know the cafe is your thing... but I think she needs the job. Ever since her husband died she's been asking for credit and she just looks so lost."

Olivia sank into one of the chairs. "I hadn't budgeted for another employee so soon. I was going to personally wait the tables and help Evelyn in the kitchen."

"And run the malt counter?"

"Yes?" She smiled sheepishly. "But realistically, we can't run it all the time with just the two of us. So, I think we do need someone else. And I've always liked Melody."

"And she has waitressing experience."

"That sounds promising."

"Why don't you call her and discuss the job and see what you think we could pay her and how many hours. We could also train her on working at the general store. Never hurts to have more backup."

"I think this is a great idea. I will call her."

"So, you aren't angry that I stepped in?"

Olivia grinned. "Mom, Parker's is your store, and the cafe is part of it. I'm grateful you let me try expanding it and opening the cafe. You believed in my dream. I won't let you down. And I think Melody Tanner will be a great worker."

Relief washed through her. At least she hadn't offended Olivia with her suggestion on who to hire. She was trying her best not to interfere in the whole cafe thing, even though she worried about it constantly. Would it be profitable? Or would Olivia's dream get crushed? But Olivia didn't need to know that.

She handed Melody's phone number to Olivia. "I better get back to work. Let me know what happens with Melody."

She hoped it worked out for all of them.

HER MOTHER WALKED AWAY, and Olivia sat at the table considering her options. She really had planned on being all things at the cafe to keep costs down. But realistically, she and Evelyn would need help. They'd already decided the cafe would be closed on Sundays, but that meant that both she and Evelyn would be working six days a week from early morning until after dinnertime. Evelyn said she was fine with the hours while they got up and running, but that was still a lot to ask.

Melody Tanner had always been friendly and would know most of the townsfolk who came in by name. That would be nice. She looked at the piece of paper with Melody's number and took out her cell phone. Might as well talk to her.

Melody answered on the second ring. "Hello?"

"Melody, this is Olivia from Parker's."

"Hi."

"So, I hear you might be interested in a job at the cafe."

"Yes, I would. I'd love one." Melody's voice brimmed with eagerness.

"Perfect. Come by tomorrow morning and we'll get you all set up. We still have a week before the opening, but you can help us with getting ready. We could start at twenty hours a week?"

"Perfect. I'll be there in the morning. And thanks, Olivia. I can really use a job. I'll work hard for you. I promise."

"I'll see you in the morning, then." She hung up her phone and realized she hadn't even spoken of pay rate. But Melody didn't seem to care. She obviously needed the job. She'd pay her a fair wage, so there was that, and Melody would get tips, too. She'd talk to her tomorrow about it.

She got up and headed to the kitchen to tell Evelyn they now would have some part-time help. She was certain Evelyn would be pleased.

A FEW DAYS later Olivia had her back to the front door of the cafe when she heard it open. She really should just lock the darn thing. So many people checking on the progress. Couldn't they read the sign? Grand Opening on Friday.

"Hey, there."

She turned to see Austin, sporting a warm smile that brought out his one dimple.

"Emily said that the malt machine is up and running. Thought I'd come by and get a malt, if that's okay. I know you aren't officially open."

"No, of course, that's okay. At the very least I need to supply you with free malts for life."

"I wouldn't say no to that." He grinned as he slid onto a barstool at the counter.

"What flavor would you like?"

"Emily suggested vanilla. Said it was the best vanilla ice cream I'd ever taste."

"Vanilla it is." She quickly and efficiently —from years of practice—made his malt.

He took one bite and nodded. "And your daughter was right. This is excellent. What's the secret to the recipe?"

She shook her head. "Nope. Family secret. Won't ever tell." But the corners of her mouth twitched with a held back smile.

"Guess I'll just have to keep coming back for more."

"Guess you will. Hope you're not the only customer we get."

"Especially since I'm not paying for this?" His eyes twinkled.

"Well, that too." She sat on the stool next to

him and swiveled to face him. "So, I was wondering. Would you like to come over for dinner tomorrow night? I'll cook. Thought you might like a home-cooked meal." Not that her cooking skills were that great, but she still felt she owed him for all he was doing.

"I'd love that."

"Great. About six?" She'd have to run to the store tonight and get what she needed and see what she could prepare in advance since she had a busy day at the cafe tomorrow. So much to do before the opening. But she did feel better that she was at least paying Austin back for his help and kindness, if only a little bit. And that was all it was. Returning the favor.

A delivery came, and she slid off the stool. "I've got to get this. Enjoy your malt, and I'll see you tomorrow."

"Thanks. See you tomorrow."

She led the delivery man into the kitchen, wishing she could stay and chat with Austin but knowing Evelyn would need help sorting out all the items in the delivery. She had to remember to text Emily too. Tell her about Austin coming to dinner tomorrow.

She wracked her mind for something easy

but nice to fix for dinner. Nothing fabulous popped into her mind. She'd have to think of something before heading out to shop this evening.

CHAPTER 14

Austin decided to walk over to Livy's the next evening. He'd gotten into the habit of walking around town whenever possible. This whole small-town thing was growing on him. From people knowing their neighbors to the ability to walk to anything he needed. He only knew two of his neighbors back in Denver. And they seemed to change constantly.

He slowed his pace, trying to time it perfectly to show up at six o'clock on the dot. He didn't want to get there too early, though he was anxious for a chance to spend time with Livy again.

He got to the door at precisely six and knocked. Emily opened the door. "Hey, Austin, come in."

He stepped inside and glanced around at his first peek inside the house. The front room was decorated in a comfortable, coastal theme. No surprise there. An overstuffed sofa and chairs made a cozy corner on one side of the room. He followed Emily through the room and into the kitchen.

Livy turned from the stove as he entered. "You're right on time. I'm just finishing this up and need to pop it in the oven for thirty minutes. It's a crabmeat casserole."

"And it's delicious," Emily added. "My fav."

"And I brought home a loaf of sourdough bread that Evelyn made today. She's been busy testing out the commercial oven."

"Sounds wonderful."

"Mom, I'm going to go do some homework. Call me when dinner's ready." Emily disappeared out of the room.

"So would you like to sit out on the lanai? We could have a beer or wine?"

"Either is fine." She had a tiny bit of flour on her cheek and he resisted the temptation to swipe it from her flushed face.

"Then just look in the fridge and pull us out two beers."

He peeked inside and found the local craft

beer he knew she liked and pulled out two bottles. He popped the caps, handed one to her, and followed her outside.

They settled into two wicker chairs facing the canal. The view was peaceful. He could imagine sitting out here all the time and just watching the water slip by, or the world slip by for that matter.

Livy kicked off her shoes. "Ah. Nice to be off my feet."

He felt a bit guilty that she'd worked all day —probably crazy busy preparing for the opening—and then came home to cook for him. "I do appreciate the offer for a home-cooked meal."

"After all you've done? It's the least I could do."

She had on a simple t-shirt dress and her hair was tied back, though a few curls had sprung loose and framed her face. She raised the bottle of beer to her lips and took a sip. He tried not to stare...

She glanced over at him and caught him watching her. "Oh, I guess I should have offered up glasses. I usually drink mine right out of the bottle."

"Bottle is fine." He took a sip to prove it and

cover up his discomfort at being caught staring at her. "Things coming along for the opening?"

"They are. Day after tomorrow. Friday. I think we have everything ready." She laughed. "At least I hope so. Evelyn is going to be busy making things tomorrow. She's going to bake the bread for the sandwiches and a few pies and sweets to serve. We don't really know what kind of business we'll get, so we might be over making things at first. I'm sure Evelyn will figure it all out as we go along."

"I bet it is hard to figure out how much you'll need of everything."

"We did get a part-time worker, though. Melody. That should help."

"If I can do anything to help, just let me know."

"As if you aren't doing enough already. Emily said you showed her how to get the ordering software installed. And you're right, it wasn't too pricey. I appreciate that." Her eyes shone with gratitude.

"I'll show her how to get the items set up and how to add new items and prices. You'll be all set for whenever you want to add in the online ordering."

Her timer went off on her phone and she

rose. "Stay, finish your beer. I'll just put the finishing touches on dinner."

She went inside, and he stared at the water slipping by the seawall behind her house. If he had a house like this on the waterway, he'd sit outside here all the time. At the far end of her property, there was a dock and boat lift with a small skiff on it. Must be nice to just walk out and take a boat out for a spin. Not that it sounded like Livy had much free time. And he didn't know a thing about boats...

Emily popped her head outside. "Dinner's ready."

He rose to go inside. The tantalizing aroma had already made his stomach growl in anticipation.

LIVY WAS PLEASED she'd thought of this delicious casserole to make. It had never failed her, and part of it she made last night, so there wasn't much left to do tonight but finish the last details of the sauce, pop it in the oven, and make a salad.

They sat at the table in the kitchen—the house was small and didn't have a dining area.

That didn't bother her because the house was just the right size for her and Emily. Though, it might have been nice to have a dining room for company tonight, not that Austin seemed to mind the casual dining.

Austin took a bite and nodded in appreciation. "This is wonderful. Seriously. Rivals any of the fancy dinners I've ever had. It's delicious."

"Thanks." She blushed slightly and pleasure spread through her at his words.

"It's an old family recipe that Mom has been making for as long as I can remember. Though I'm pretty sure my ancestors made the pasta shells by hand." Emily reached for a piece of bread.

"So, I guess I won't ask for this recipe, either." He grinned.

"You can ask... but don't expect an answer." Olivia relaxed at the easy dinner bantering.

They ate their meal chatting about the cafe and the new software. Emily excitedly told them about all the social media posts she'd been making and still planned to make. She'd been taking lots of photos with her handy-dandy fancy new cell phone her dad had gotten her.

Not that it still bothered her.

Much.

But she did love seeing her daughter so animated.

As they finished the meal, Emily jumped up and grabbed her plate. "It was great, Mom, but I've got to run. Meeting my study group. We have that big science exam tomorrow. I won't be late." Emily set her dishes in the sink with a clatter and within minutes had swept out the door in the whirlwind that was always her daughter.

Austin leaned back in his chair. "That was a great meal. Just great."

"Thank you." She stood and picked up her dishes.

Austin immediately jumped up and grabbed his plate.

"No, sit. I'll clear the table."

"Nonsense. I'll help." Austin brought the dishes over while she rinsed them and placed them in the dishwasher.

She looked around at the picked up kitchen and turned to him. "So, would you like another drink out on the lanai?"

"I would."

They brought beer out with them and settled back on the chairs. The breeze had shifted slightly and filtered in through the screening. A mother duck and her brood swam past in the canal.

Austin let out a long sigh. "Man, I could get used to this. It's so peaceful here."

"It is. I just love living on the canal system. Maybe after things calm down from all the crazy of the opening, I could take you out cruising the canals." She caught herself. "I mean, if you're still here in town."

"I'll be here for a while longer. I'm in no hurry to leave." His mouth curved into one of his irresistible smiles.

A smile that made her pulse quicken, though she firmly ignored the feeling of it racing through her veins. And ignored the smile, too. Totally.

Austin set his beer down and leaned toward her, his eyes intense. "I know we said that we wouldn't date. But... I really do enjoy spending time with you. I hope that's okay."

"Yes, it's fine. I mean, I like spending time with you, too." A lot. Like a lot, lot. But she didn't say that out loud.

"Though I'm pretty sure the twins still think we're an item. I guess we should clue them in on our change of status." He winked as he leaned back in his chair.

"Won't matter. They've made up their minds." She laughed. "No one changes the minds of the Jenkins twins."

CHAPTER 15

Austin didn't really mind if the Jenkins twins or the whole town thought he was dating Livy. Unless that caused problems for her. Because, to tell the truth, he'd love to be officially dating her. Though Jesse's warning did still nag at him.

But Livy intrigued him. He loved the musical tones of her laugh and the way one side of her mouth quirked up when she was trying to hide a smile. He loved the way she blushed if he gave her a compliment. He—he should stop listing off everything he loved about her.

Ignoring his thoughts, he concentrated on his beer while they chatted about the opening of the cafe. Glancing at his watch, he thought he should probably leave. She had a big day tomorrow to finish getting ready for Friday's opening.

But he really wanted to stay. So he did, and they chatted for a while longer.

Livy finally glanced at her watch. "I guess I should call it an evening. I have to be at the cafe early tomorrow." She rose.

He got up and stood beside her, sorry to see the evening come to a close. "Didn't mean to keep you up so late."

She laughed her charming laugh. "It's not late. I just go to bed early since I have to be up so early."

He followed her inside, dropped his bottle into the bin she said was recycling, and followed her to the front door. She stepped outside on the front step with him, standing ever so close. The faint scent of lavender enticed him, teased him. He swallowed. Hard.

"I—" he cleared his throat. "I had a nice time. And it was a wonderful meal. Thank you."

"I—*we*—enjoyed having you."

He stared at her eyes, mesmerized by them as she tilted her face up to him. He knew it was foolish, but he was going to kiss her. Wanted to kiss her. Needed to kiss her. He leaned forward just slightly.

"Hey, Mom. Austin." Emily came hurrying up the walk.

Where had she come from?

"Uh, hi, Emily." He recovered from staring at Livy. Kind of. Disappointment swelled through him, but he knew it was best to leave. At least Emily hadn't caught him kissing her mother. "Well, it's late. I should go."

"Night, Austin." Emily stood beside Livy now, and Livy threaded her arm around her daughter.

"Bye. And thanks. Had a great time." He turned and walked down the stairs. Sorry for the missed opportunity. And sad that he hadn't actually kissed her.

Now he would wonder all night long what it would have been like.

"He was going to kiss you." Emily leaned against her as Austin walked away down the street.

"What? You're crazy." Her voice was firm. She sounded confident. But *was* Em crazy? For a brief moment, she *had* thought he was going to kiss her. And she'd wanted him to.

145

"Nope, I'm not crazy. He likes you. I can tell." Emily grinned and turned to slip inside.

Livy sank down on the worn top step of the porch, staring into the distance where Austin had disappeared. She was pretty sure Emily was right. There had been an electrical connection with Austin as they stood there on the porch. He had to have been feeling the same thing, right?

But what were they doing?

And she had Emily to consider. They didn't need to get close to Austin... or even overly friendly... just for him to leave. Too many people had left them. Her own father had left. Then Brett had left and rarely visited Emily. She wasn't going to add another person to the list.

She stared out into the darkness, broken only by the scattered streetlights. It would be best if she just didn't see Austin again. There, a decision was made. She felt better.

Sort of.

She sighed.

No, she felt worse.

But of course, she'd see him some. He'd be around town. He was working with Emily. She owed him free ice cream...

Emily poked her head out the door. "Mom, you're overthinking things again. Wouldn't hurt you to date him while he's in town." The door closed again with a thud.

A small smile crossed her face as she rose from the steps. Maybe her daughter was right. She was just overthinking this whole thing. It was okay to just have a good time with someone, wasn't it?

CHAPTER 16

Olivia couldn't believe Heather had talked her into meeting her at Brewster's the day before the grand opening of the cafe. But Heather had said she was sure it would be ages until she'd talk her into it again since Olivia would be so busy. And Heather was right, it probably would be ages, so she'd obliged her cousin a quick coffee this morning.

She spotted Heather sitting at a table by the edge of the water with two coffees in front of her. Perfect. She'd just drink hers and hurry to the cafe.

"Morning." Heather slid one of the mugs across the table.

"Good morning. Can't believe you talked

me into this. I bet your mom is already at The Sea Glass, hard at work."

"She is. I texted her this morning."

"I should be there."

"Relax and have your coffee. Who knows when we'll be able to do this again. As it is, I barely see you anymore."

"We've been busy with the opening." She shrugged and took a sip of the coffee. Still piping hot. Maybe if she threw some ice into it, the coffee would cool down enough for her to drink it quickly.

"I just miss you."

"I know. I miss you, too. Things will settle down." Sometime. And she didn't think that sometime was anytime soon.

"So... I heard that you asked Austin over for dinner last night."

"How did you..."

"I ran into Emily and she told me he was coming to dinner. Is there anything you want to tell me?"

"No, I was just repaying him for all he's done for Emily. And he taught her how to install the ordering system for the cafe. And how to do the social media. And, well, lots of stuff." If she said it often enough, maybe someone would believe her. She was just repaying his kindness. Maybe if she said it enough, *she'd* believe it.

"The twins have been spreading the rumor you're dating." Heather cocked her head and raised a brow questioningly.

"No... we're not. We specifically decided not to. I mean, he'll leave soon. And Emily—"

"Don't use Emily as an excuse. She's a big girl. And she doesn't care if you date or who you date as long as he's not a serial killer or something."

Olivia leaned back in her chair and sighed. "I know. She told me I should date him. But I already told him that we shouldn't. And gave him some good reasons, too."

Heather rolled her eyes. "Come on. Date the guy. What will it hurt?"

"He'll be leaving soon."

"I'm not asking you to get serious or marry him. Just go out and have fun."

"But I'm so busy right now." She shook her head.

"All the more reason that you should take some breaks and enjoy yourself. Life can't all be about work." Heather pinned her with a don't-argue-with-me stare.

She leaned forward with her elbows on the

table. "Well... I did think he was going to kiss me last night."

"Well, that's a tidbit of news." Heather grinned. "Why didn't he?"

"Emily walked up right then."

"That girl has some really bad timing." Heather took a sip of coffee and set the mug down. "But... did you want him to kiss you?"

Her silly pulse quickened just being asked that question. She shrugged nonchalantly, trying to cover. "Maybe."

Heather laughed. "You *did* want him to kiss you. I can tell."

"Okay, I confess. I did want him to. There, are you happy?" She swept up her mug and took a swallow, glaring at her cousin.

Heather's lips curved into a self-satisfied grin. "So, do you think he'll ask you out again? Or you could ask him out."

"I'm not going to ask him out."

"Why not?"

"Because..." She sighed. "Because I want *him* to ask me out. But I don't think he will because we already discussed not dating. We're just being... friendly."

"I don't know what I'm going to do with

you." Heather scowled. "Ask him. The next time you see him. Promise me."

"Maybe." She refused to commit. "I really should go now. Aunt Evelyn needs me at the cafe. We have so much to do before tomorrow."

"Here, I'll walk out with you. I'm glad we at least got a little time together." Heather took her last swallow and rose.

They headed down the wharf, passing just a few people in the early morning hours. Other coffee drinkers, most likely.

Heather grabbed her elbow. "Don't look now, but the twins are approaching."

Olivia looked left and right for a way to escape, but they were too far from any of the cut-throughs to the back walkways. "Just what I don't need."

The twins bustled up to them. "Hello, Parker girls. How are you doing on this lovely morning?"

"Just fine. In a bit of a hurry though." Maybe she could cut them off at the pass.

"And how is that handsome Austin doing? He's a mighty fine catch, you know," one of the twins said. Would she ever be able to tell them apart?

"I haven't *caught* him. We're not even dating," she insisted.

"You went to dinner. That's a date." Both twins nodded vigorously.

Why was she even bothering to argue with them? "We've got to run. Have the cafe grand opening tomorrow."

"We're so excited about Parker's Cafe opening."

"Sea Glass Cafe," she corrected them.

"Right. We'll be there."

"For sure." The twins seemed to finish each other's thoughts.

"Uh, great. I guess I'll see you there." She grasped Heather's elbow to hurry her along.

Heather laughed as they got a short distance from the Jenkins sisters. "You'll never convince them you're not dating Austin, so go ahead and ask him out."

"I only have time to worry about the cafe now," she insisted. Although she was a bit tempted to ask him out. Maybe. Because both Heather and Emily had said she should date him. She shook her head, cleared her thoughts.

The cafe. The opening. Nothing else mattered right now. Certainly not her dating life.

CHAPTER 17

Barry stood with Delbert in the lobby of The Cabot, waiting for Donna to show up for their dinner date.

"You've done a great job with helping get The Cabot remodeled and up and running," Delbert said. "Everything is moving along smoothly now."

"It seems to be. I have to admit, this was one of my favorite jobs."

"Glad to hear that." Delbert gave him a warm smile. "I admit, I'll miss having you around all the time."

Yes, there was that. The job was almost finished now, and it would be time to move on...

He had liked working for Del. The job had its challenges and mix-ups, but overall things had gone well. The Cabot was a remarkable, charming hotel now, restored to her former glory with necessary updates.

"Good evening, Delbert."

They both turned at the sound of Camille's voice. She stood grasping the arm of Senator Miller, who looked a bit shocked. As if stunned to have such a beautiful woman on his arm.

"Hello there, gentlemen," the senator said.

"Herbert here insisted we come to dinner at the hotel. He hasn't seen it since you bought it." Camille graced the senator with a smile. "I wanted to go to Sarasota, but... well, we like to keep the senator happy, don't we?"

Actually, Barry didn't care if the senator was happy or not... Why had he insisted on bringing Camille to Del's hotel?

"Glad to have you, Senator." Delbert reached out and shook the man's hand. "Enjoy your meal." His voice was steady and cordial.

"Oh, I'm sure we will, won't we, darling?" Camille actually batted her eyelashes at good old Herbert.

The senator led Camille away, and Barry raised an eyebrow. "That was surprising."

"What, that she's dating the senator?"

Delbert turned from watching them walking away.

"No, that she'd come here." He was aware that she'd probably come to flaunt her new man in front of Delbert, even though he was fairly certain Del didn't care who Camille dated.

"She's free to go where she wants. With who she wants." Del shrugged, then frowned. "Though I admit I'd rather she'd pick about anywhere else in the world to dine than one of my hotels."

Barry laughed. "But then she couldn't show off her new guy."

Del glanced in the direction of Camille and the senator. "Maybe he'll have better luck with dating her than I did."

Barry didn't detect one hint of jealousy or regret in Del's tone of voice. Maybe there was even a bit of relief showing on his face.

"I should go. I have a phone call to make. You enjoy your dinner with Donna."

"I'm sure I will."

DONNA STOOD in the entrance to the dining room at The Cabot Hotel. She'd been tempted to cancel with everything going on with the cafe's opening, but Olivia had insisted that she still go.

She scanned the tables, looking for Barry.

"Hey, beautiful." Barry's voice came from behind her.

She turned to see his welcoming smile. Her heart did a silly school-girl flip. He leaned forward and kissed her quickly on the cheek. "I've missed you."

"I've missed you, too." She could still feel the warmth of his lips on her cheek after he pulled away. She looked around, wondering if anyone had seen the kiss. Not that she minded. The town was well aware by now that she was seeing him.

"I was afraid you'd cancel with the opening tomorrow."

"Olivia insisted I come. She and Evelyn will probably be there until who knows how late."

"I, for one, am glad she insisted." He gave her another smile that sent her heart doing double beats in her chest.

He took her arm, and they got a table for two by the windows overlooking Moonbeam Bay. She tried not to stare at him. He looked especially handsome tonight in a blue button-down shirt that lit up his sky-blue eyes. She got lost in the tones of his voice while he regaled her of stories of the hotel and the finishing touches on the remodel while they ate their dinner. She so enjoyed spending time with him, talking with him.

"So, would you like to go sit out on the porch for a bit? Watch the sunset?" Barry offered as they finished their meal.

"That sounds lovely."

They took their wine out to the porch and settled into a rocking loveseat facing the water. He wrapped his arm around her shoulders, and she leaned against him. The rocker slowly swayed back and forward.

"The last of the sunlight hitting the water? It sparkles like diamonds, doesn't it?" She smiled up at him.

"It does," he agreed. "Very pretty view here."

The sun slowly sank lower, and the sparkles faded away. The moment was perfect. Just sitting here watching the beauty before them. They sat quietly watching the evening sky erupt in brilliant colors of the sunset.

"I've been meaning to talk to you." Barry's

voice interrupted the quiet, and he stopped the gentle rocking motion.

"Oh? What about?"

"My job is almost finished here at The Cabot."

She closed her eyes, willing him not to continue. Not go on to the inevitable next words.

"I've gotten another job offer and I'm going to go check on it next week."

She pulled away from him slightly, bracing herself. "Where is this new project?"

"It's in... Oregon. On the coast."

A person couldn't get much further away from Moonbeam than that. She looked down at her hands now, noticing a bit of chipped polish and the way her watch was twisted off-center on her wrist. She twisted it back into place. "Well, we knew your job would end here sometime."

He reached over and placed his hand gently under her chin, tilting her face up to look directly at him. "The job has ended... but my feelings for you haven't. I have to go check out this job on Monday, but I'll be back at the end of the week."

She didn't want to ask the question. Didn't

want to think about it. But it needed to be asked. "And then what?"

His forehead creased. "And then we'll have to work something out. I don't plan on just walking away from... this."

"What *is* this?"

"I'm not sure, but I know that I care about you. Deeply. I love spending time with you, talking to you."

She reached up, touched his face, and he covered her hand with his. "I enjoy spending time with you, too." She'd gotten used to seeing him almost every day. A coffee here, a dinner there. And most evenings he came over to her house to sit out on the point and they'd have a glass of wine or chamomile tea. She would miss that.

"We'll figure this out, Donna. We have to."

She nodded, not daring to speak.

He pulled her close again, and they sat not talking, each of them lost in their thoughts. She finally pulled away. "We should probably get going. I have an early day tomorrow."

He rose and held out a hand for her, pulling her gently to her feet. "We should, then."

They headed through the hotel and out to the long circle drive in front of the hotel. Barry laughed softly. "Remember when I couldn't find my way around town and you had to lead me back to my rental house?"

"I do."

"Quite fortuitous that I rented the house right next to yours."

"It was." Fate was sly like that sometimes. Found ways to drop someone right into your life.

He stopped under the lamplight and turned to look down at her. "Donna, we'll figure this out. We'll work something out."

Maybe. But then, maybe it would get too complicated with a long-distance relationship. Or he'd get tired of traveling back to see her. She couldn't just go jet-setting across the country to see him. She had to be here for Parker's, especially with the cafe just opening.

She wanted to reassure him that things would work out. That it would all be okay. But somehow, she just wasn't able to. She just nodded again.

He sighed and took her hand. His hand was warm and comforting wrapped around hers. She glanced down at their grasp. She'd miss this, too. The little things. Like holding his hand.

They continued walking home in silence

until they reached her front steps. "I'll let you go in, then. I know you have to be up early."

She had planned on asking him to sit outside and have some tea. But she did have to get up early. But maybe he was pulling back now. In preparation for the new stage of their relationship?

He wrapped his arms around her, pulled her close, and kissed her gently. She slid her arms around his waist and leaned against him after the kiss. She'd miss this too. His kisses. His holding her.

Loneliness swept through her, which was ridiculous because she was right here in his arms. She pulled away and looked up into his face, seeing the same emotions she was feeling flit across his features. He gave her a small smile. "Good night."

"Night, Barry." He walked over to his cottage and waved one time before he slipped into the house.

She opened the door and entered her dark house. She headed to her room without bothering to turn on the lights.

CHAPTER 18

Olivia had lost count of how many people had come to the cafe today for its grand opening. She hadn't had a moment to so much as take a breath for hours. Evelyn was working at a feverish pace in the kitchen, and Melody ping-ponged between helping in the kitchen and waiting on tables. At this rate, she'd need to hire even more help. That is, if things kept up like this and it wasn't just people wanting to see the cafe since it was so new. But the crowd today had outdone her highest projections.

If she survived the hectic pace...

Emily hurried into the cafe, her school bag slung off one shoulder. "Mom, look how busy we are. This is great."

"How was school?"

"Fine. But I'm going to grab some photos of this and post on social media. Then I'll help out wherever you need me."

"Thanks. It's been busy like this all day." And who knew what the dinner rush might look like.

She found out soon enough. Every table was taken, and people milled around the store, waiting for their turn to sit. That was an unexpected benefit as they bought items at the general store while they waited. Emily took names for the waitlist, then went to find them in the store when tables opened up.

Heather walked into the cafe, took one look around, and hurried up to her. "You guys are packed."

"Been like this most of the day."

"I'm going to head to the kitchen and help Mom."

"I'm sure she can use it."

She popped into the kitchen a few minutes later to get the next order and looked over at Evelyn. "How you holding up?"

"I'm doing okay. Wow, we've been busy. So happy I prepared extra. And I was glad to see Heather show up to help."

Heather looked up from slicing a fresh loaf of sourdough bread. "I'm thinking you two are going to have to hire more help."

"I was thinking the same thing. We'll see how it goes for a few days and see if things settle down."

"I'm going to come in and help until you figure it out."

"Oh, Heather, you don't have to do that," Evelyn protested.

"But I want to. I did invest in the cafe, you know. I want you guys to succeed. And by the looks of this crowd, you will."

"Aunt Evelyn's soup is a big hit. So is her turkey and bacon sandwich. Everyone keeps talking about the sauce on it."

"That was one of the family recipes." Evelyn pointed to the ever-present binder of recipes with the weathered and faded original recipes copied and printed out for keeping here at the cafe. The original recipe cards were safe at home.

"You almost make me want to learn to make all those recipes." Olivia grinned as she grabbed the two plates waiting for her. She hurried back out with the food.

"Olivia, dear, this soup is excellent." One of

the Jenkins twins stopped her as she walked past their table.

"I'm glad you like it."

"We're happy for a new place to eat in town. Just delicious," the other twin said. "We'll be back again for sure. I predict the Parker Cafe will be a big success."

"Sea Glass Cafe," she gently corrected.

"Right. We'll be back soon."

"And we'll be glad to see you." Who knew she could be happy about seeing the twins again? Usually, she did her best to avoid them. But a paying customer? Two, actually? She'd never turn that away.

The dinner rush was just beginning to ebb when Austin showed up. "Hey, Austin."

"Couldn't miss your grand opening," he said as he sat down at a table.

She couldn't help noticing her pulse quicken at just seeing him. Heather's voice taunted her. *Ask him out the next time you see him.*

She didn't have time to think about that now. She handed him the printed menu and pointed to the specials on a large chalkboard over the counter. "I'll be back to get your order."

She checked out two tables of customers

and came back to Austin's table, glancing around to see there were finally empty tables scattered around. She glanced at her watch. Thirty minutes until closing time. She couldn't wait to get off her feet.

"Did you decide what you want to order?"

"I did. I think I'll try the soup of the day and the turkey and bacon sandwich. Who can resist bacon?" He grinned at her.

"Wise choice."

She was soon back with his order and checked out two more customers. Only Austin and one other table left.

Emily walked past with an armload of dirty dishes from clearing some tables. "Want me to flip the sign to closed?"

"Yes, do that."

"I'm going to help get these dishes run before I head out. I'm meeting some friends."

"Thanks for all your help today."

Emily dumped the dishes in the kitchen, went back to the door, and flipped the sign over. She checked out the last customer except for Austin and headed back to the kitchen.

Olivia headed over to Austin. "Would you like some dessert?"

"I would love some ice cream. Care to join me?"

She looked around at the empty tables. "I could for a few minutes. Would love to get off my feet. It's been quite the day."

She got ice cream for both of them and sat down across from him. "Ah, that feels good."

"Busy day, huh? I saw some pics that Emily posted online. She did a great job, by the way."

"We had people in here all day long. Which is good, I guess. I just hope they keep coming back and it wasn't just a grand opening thing."

"The food was delicious. I'm sure they'll be back." He took a bite of his ice cream. "And the ice cream never disappoints, either.

She finally had a glimmer of hope that she was actually going to pull this off. That the cafe was going to show a profit. And at this rate, it would be sooner than she expected. Relief washed through her. She realized she'd been half-afraid that hardly anyone would show up today.

Now, if they just showed up again. And again.

Heather came out and cleared the last table. "Hi, Austin."

"Hi, Heather. So you came to help out today, too?"

"Can't let my cousin have all the fun." She laughed as she held up the tray of dirty dishes. She moved behind Austin's back and nodded at him, her eyes wide. *Ask him.* She mouthed the words, then turned to head back to the kitchen.

Olivia gathered her courage, still not sure this was the right thing to do, but Heather would bug her relentlessly until she did. "So… I was wondering…"

He looked across the table, an eyebrow raised.

"Would you… I mean." *So cool, Olivia. So cool.* "Would you like to go out? On a date, I mean. With me." Could she sound any more awkward?

His eyes widened in surprise. "Yes. Yes, I would."

"Oh, good. Great." She sat back. There, she'd asked him. Heather would be so proud of her.

"When?"

When? She hadn't thought that far through things. "Uh… soon?"

He grinned. "How soon?"

She realized she didn't have any idea when she'd have some time off. Not until the cafe got running.

"How about Sunday? I saw you're closed on Sunday," Austin suggested.

She was fairly sure she'd be exhausted by Sunday, but it did seem like the best time to go out. "Sure, Sunday would be great."

"And where are we going?"

She really hadn't thought this whole thing out very well... "Uh... where would you like to go?"

"Dinner?"

"Sure, that sounds good."

"Where do you want to go? The dining room at The Cabot again?"

"Ah... how about Jimmy's on the wharf again?"

"Sounds good to me. Loved it there. Want me to swing by and pick you up?"

"How about I just meet you there? I don't know if I'll be at home or maybe at the store or cafe."

"Six work?" he asked.

"That sounds perfect."

There, she'd done it. Not only asked him out

on a date, but it was all planned and set up. That should keep Heather from bugging her. That was the only reason she'd asked him... and maybe if she said that enough, she'd begin to believe that big fat lie.

CHAPTER 19

Heather strolled along the wharf with her mother on Sunday evening. She'd insisted on taking her mom out to give her a little break. Her mom had worked long, hard hours the last few weeks leading up to the cafe opening and deserved a little pampering.

"You didn't need to do this, but it is lovely to get out for a change," her mother said as they headed toward Portside Grill, one of her mother's favorite restaurants.

The wharf was busy this evening with people out getting dinner at the many restaurants and cafes scattered along the pier. They slowly wound their way through the crowds, stopping to look in some of the shop windows along the main walkway.

She looked down through the crowds and stopped short. Her mother paused and looked at her. "Heather?"

"Ah... Mom." She nodded ahead of them. "It looks like Father is here at the wharf. And... he's not alone."

Her mother turned, her gaze sweeping the crowd until she saw him. "I'd heard he finally got back in town. I believe he moved back into the house with his new woman."

"She looks more like a girl to me."

"She's just a bit older than you."

She looked at the couple walking toward them. "Do you want to leave? We'll go somewhere else."

"I'm not going to let him chase me away from a nice night out with my daughter." Her mother squared her shoulders, her eyes flashing with determination.

Heather stepped beside her and wrapped an arm around her mother's waist. "Then on we go." If her mother was brave enough to confront the man, so was she. Even if she'd spent most of her life avoiding him...

They continued down the walkway until Heather knew the exact moment her Father saw them. He paused, looked down at the woman on his arm, and said something to her. The woman looked up quickly and stared at them. Her father began walking toward them again.

"Isn't this just perfect?" Heather whispered to her mom.

"Evelyn, Heather." Her father stopped when he reached them.

"Darren," her mother said.

"Father." Her voice held an edge of anger and distrust, though it appeared he didn't notice. Not that her father noticed much of anything about her, so this wasn't new.

"This is Lacey."

He introduced his girlfriend. Lacey the homewrecker. And it appeared she had no last name. Probably hoping to get her father's last name soon...

"And Lacey, you know, my wi—I mean Evelyn." He didn't even have the good grace to blush.

"Yes, hello." Lacey bobbed her head of golden curls while she held possessively onto her father's arm as if she was going to lose him if he talked to his *wife* for long enough. And she still *was* his wife, in spite of her father acting like he was already divorced.

"Evelyn, I'm still waiting for those signed

papers." He eyed her mother, giving her his world-famous don't-argue-with-me glare. The one that always worked for him in business.

"Not ready to sign them."

She almost laughed out loud at her mother's statement. Good for her.

"I don't know why you're making this so difficult." He took a step forward, but her mom didn't back away.

Her mom glanced pointedly at Lacey and said, "I don't think this is the time to discuss the matter. And if you have anything to say to me about it, it would be better if you contacted my lawyer."

"You're just being silly. Difficult. You know I don't like it when you're difficult. Just sign the papers."

"Father, you heard her. And she's right. This is not the time for the discussion." Heather stepped forward, facing her father directly and ignoring the woman clinging to his arm.

"Stay out of it. This doesn't concern you," her father barked at her.

"Right, my parents' divorce doesn't concern me." She rolled her eyes at him, knowing full well that it irritated him when she did that.

His face reddened. *Ah, she'd got to him*. Good.

He gave one more glare at her mother. "Sign those papers. Immediately. Stop this nonsense." Then he dismissed her with barely a nod. "Let's go now, Lacey." He grabbed Lacey's arm and steered her around them.

"Bye, Father. Great to see you," she called out merrily after them. "Jerk," she said under her breath.

Her mother let out a long breath. "Well, he's as charming as ever, isn't he?"

"He's... he's not worth our time thinking of names to call him. You okay?"

"I'm fine. I *will* be fine. I actually can't wait to be divorced from him."

"But you're going to take your time signing those papers, aren't you?" A grin began to spread across her face as she watched her mother.

Her mother's mouth lifted in an amused smile. "Yes, I do think I will wait just a bit. Now that he commanded I sign them immediately. It's not going to happen. Besides, my lawyer still wants to make some changes to the agreement."

"Father isn't going to like that." She grinned even wider.

"He won't. But I'm done worrying about what your father likes or doesn't like. And he's given me one too many orders, too."

"He's given you hundreds of orders too many. He treats you like you work for him, not like you're his wife. You should wait months to sign those papers."

"He no longer gets what he wants, when he wants it. I'm finished with that."

She looked at her mother in admiration. "Mom, you're an incredibly strong woman and I'm really proud of you."

Her mom's eyes filled with gratitude. "Thank you. That means a lot to me to hear that."

"So, you ready to go to Portside Grill? We'll order a bottle of champagne and toast to the strong Parker women."

"Let's."

"You know, Grace Parker would be very proud that she had such a strong great-granddaughter like you. Parker women are made of tough stuff." She laughed, glad her mother had taken the confrontation with her father in stride. But her mother was different these days. Stronger. More confident. And one of the hardest working women she'd ever met.

Her mother hugged her. "And she'd be proud of a successful, beautiful, caring great-great-granddaughter like you. And I'm lucky to have you as my daughter."

"As long as we're talking about Parker women... " She pulled back slightly from her mother's embrace. "I have something to tell you."

"What?"

"I've legally changed my last name to Parker. I haven't told you because I didn't want to hurt your feelings. It wasn't because of you. Because of anything you did."

Her mother's eyes widened, then a small smile crossed her face. "Trying to disassociate yourself from your father?"

"Yes. And I'd taken Heather Parker for my artist name and then it just finally seemed to suit me better. Are you disappointed?"

"No, not a bit." She shrugged. "A matter of fact, I wouldn't mind losing the Carlson name myself." Her mother's smile widened. "Let's go have that champagne."

They headed to the restaurant, their spirits surprisingly high after such a tense confrontation. Heather rode along on a high that nothing could stop her mother now. She

181

was going to get what she wanted and what she deserved.

CHAPTER 20

Livy met Austin at Jimmy's where he was already waiting for her at a table by the water. She smiled when she saw he'd ordered her favorite craft beer and it was waiting for her. She climbed onto the stool across from him. "I see you have my drink waiting."

"Now that I know what you like." He smiled, his eyes twinkling. "And it's become one of my favorites now, too."

She glanced down to the far end of the deck and waved to the musician who was setting up for the evening. "That's Dave Post. He's really great. Love his music."

"I'm looking forward to it then." Austin glanced at the menu. "I'm having a hard time deciding what to try this time."

"Try the she-crab soup. It's great. And then anything else. Everything is good here." She laughed. "That's probably why it's my favorite spot to come eat. Love the atmosphere, the view, the music."

"I can see why it's your favorite."

They ordered their meals and Austin pushed his beer to the side, leaning closer. "So, how was Saturday at the cafe? Still busy?"

"Crazy busy. And Evelyn and I worked about half of today getting things ready for tomorrow. Trying to stay ahead of things."

"You going to hire more help?"

"Probably. If things stay this busy. Which I hope they do." She gave him a sheepish smile. "I'm still afraid I'll wake up one morning and find out this is just the whole first-opening thing going on."

"I doubt it. The food is great. Location is great."

"Mom said sales are up at the general store too. Not surprised with more people milling around in there waiting for a table."

"You must be proud of all your hard work. That it's paying off."

She blushed. "I am kind of proud." Actually, she was tremendously proud, but that sounded boastful. "I think the cafe turned out really nice. The decorating turned out better than I expected. It's got a beach vibe and I think it says comfortable and homey. And people love Evelyn's cooking."

"So are you going to work six days a week from morning until after the dinner rush? Because I'm not seeing how I'm going to be able to get you out on another date at that rate. Or maybe I'll only get to see you on Sundays. Though it appears you worked most of today, too."

She laughed. "We're just barely into *this* date."

"I was glad you asked me out." His voice took on an earnest tone. "Really glad. I know you said that you needed to be careful because of Emily."

"It appears that Emily is your biggest fan. She told me to go out with you."

"I knew I liked that girl." He grinned at her.

She looked over at him, pausing for a moment, wondering if she should continue. *What the heck.* "I'm glad I asked you out too. You're easy to talk to. I have fun when we're together."

"Glad to hear that because I really enjoy spending time with you, too."

Warmth spread through her at his admission.

Before she could say anything else the Jenkins twins walked by their table and stopped. Both had wide, knowing smiles on their faces. "So, here you two are again."

"They're having dinner together again. That's a date, right, Jillian?"

"Ah, ladies. Good to see you. Yes, this is actually a date." Austin looked over at her and grinned.

Livy kicked him under the table.

"Of course it is. I'm so glad to see you two getting along. Livy is such a sweet girl." Jackie bobbed her head vigorously. "She needs to date more. And to take some time for herself, away from Parker's Cafe."

"Sea Glass Cafe," she corrected, but she was beginning to think it was hopeless.

They both ignored the correction. "We'll leave you two lovebirds to your dinner." The two women walked away to a table at the far end of the seating area.

"You're impossible." She turned to Austin. "You like to encourage them."

"I do kind of like it." His mouth spread into a wide, teasing smile. "What's a little town gossip, anyway?"

"It won't be a *little* gossip now. They'll announce to every single person they see." She tried to look annoyed. And failed. "At least until some bigger gossip comes along."

"So you don't really mind?"

"Might have been a better thing to ask me before you stirred things up." She tried to look stern.

"I'll be better next time. I promise." But she didn't really buy his innocent expression.

"So, there'll be a next time?" Her eyebrow raised with the question.

"Another date, for sure. And maybe we'll choose a place where we don't run into the twins."

Olivia laughed. "But they are everywhere."

"Seems like it." He grinned at her again.

She was totally enjoying herself and his company and their teasing. They finished their meal, and she led him out of the restaurant, careful to choose a route that didn't take them past the twins.

He took her hand in his and they headed down the walkway. She tried to concentrate on every little detail. The warmth of his hand, the twinkle of the lights strung above them, the tone of his voice as he chatted with her as they walked along.

"Livy, Austin." She paused at the sound of Heather calling their names. Heather and Evelyn came walking up.

"Hey, did you guys have dinner on the wharf, too?" she asked.

"We did. At Portside Grill." Heather darted her eyes at Austin holding her hand and a small smile crept across her cousin's face.

She rolled her eyes at Heather.

"It was wonderful," Evelyn added, unaware of the unspoken cousin-speak going on between them.

"And guess who we ran into?" Heather's eyes narrowed for a moment. "Father and his new girlfriend, Lacey."

"Ouch. How did that go?" Livy glanced at Evelyn, wondering what it must have been like for her to see her soon-to-be ex with his new woman.

"As well as could be expected. He ordered Mom around and told her to sign the divorce papers. Mom stood her ground."

"Good for you, Aunt Evelyn."

"I admit to being quite tired of being bullied by him. Anyway, enough of this talk." Evelyn turned to Austin. "Did you enjoy your dinner?"

"Very much so."

"Glad you talked Livy into taking the night off."

"The same could be said to you." Livy eyed her aunt.

Evelyn laughed. "We're just two over-worked people... who happen to love what they do."

Olivia smiled. "And I do love it."

"We should let you go," Heather said pointedly. "Mom, let's duck into this shop. I want to see if they have any of my illustrations in here."

"I'll see you tomorrow, Evelyn."

"Bright and early." Evelyn and Heather went into a nearby shop.

"I take it your Aunt is going through a hard divorce," Austin said.

"Yes, she is. My uncle is... a jerk. A creep. A... never mind. Do you think I still have to call him my uncle after they're divorced?"

"I think that would be totally up to you."

"He was a horrible father to Heather and has always treated Aunt Evelyn like she was some kind of possession or something. Never gave her any credit for everything she did for him. Anyway... let's just say I'm not a fan of his. Never have been. Never will." Why was she explaining all this to Austin? He probably didn't want to hear all her family's problems.

"I'm sorry." He gave her a sympathetic and supportive look. And his simple remark was just what she needed to hear.

AUSTIN CONTINUED to hold Livy's hand as they left Evelyn and Heather behind. He was sorry to hear about Evelyn's troubles. Family dynamics were often complicated. He was very grateful that his parents were still together, and that he hadn't experienced anything like what Heather must be going through with her folks splitting.

They walked on in silence for a bit, Livy obviously lost in thought. But he was fine with that. Their silence was a comfortable one, and he had thoughts of his own that rambled through his mind. Like when the twins had said that Livy should be dating more. He didn't want her dating *more*. He wanted her to date *him*. And it was way too early in the relationship to be thinking this, but he didn't want her dating someone else. It would... bother him. He knew that.

He was really enjoying spending time with her. He'd been so excited when she asked him to go out again. He'd been respecting her wishes before when she said she didn't want to date because of Emily. He was thankful for her change of heart. Or thankful for Emily pushing her mom into going out with him again. Whatever the reason, he'd take it.

But he still heard Jesse's voice in his head. "Don't hurt her."

He had no plans to. None at all. He just wanted...

What did he want?

Yes, his mind was a jumble of thoughts.

As they got to the end of the pier, he stopped. "May I walk you home?"

"You don't have to." She looked up at him and his breath caught at the simple smile she gave him.

"But I want to. I'm not ready for this night to end." *How's that for some honesty?*

She looked at him for a moment, then nodded. "I'm not ready for it to end either."

Her admission made his heart sing. He

squeezed her hand, and she smiled up at him *again*. And his breath caught *again*.

They headed down the sidewalk toward her home. Unfortunately, even though he slowed his pace, they reached her house way too soon.

They climbed the stairs and stood for a moment. He gathered his thoughts. His words. "So..."

She looked at him expectantly.

The heck with wavering.

He reached out and gently touched her chin, tilted her face up, leaned down, and kissed her. Her hands grasped his shoulders, and he pulled her closer.

He finally pulled back, searching her face. Her face that held a slightly bemused look.

"I... wasn't expecting that."

"But it was okay?" he asked hurriedly.

"It was more than okay. It was really nice." She grinned, stood on tiptoe, and kissed him.

He took her into his arms and they stood like that, kissing and holding each other. Minutes slipped by, and still, they stood together in the moonlight.

"I—I should probably go in." She finally pulled back slightly. "Would you... would you like to come in for a bit?" She absentmindedly ran her fingers over her lips. He didn't think she even noticed she did it.

"I'd like that a lot." He still wasn't ready for the evening to end. And if he could get another kiss from her, so much the better.

She opened the door and led him inside, through the front room, and into the kitchen where she stopped suddenly and he ran into her, surprised by her unexpected pause.

Emily was sitting at a table with a man. "Mom, look, Dad came to town to see us."

Livy stiffened in front of him. "Hello, Brett."

"Hey, Livs."

Livs? He had his own pet name for her?

"And guess what?" Emily's eyes shone, and she jumped up from the table. "Dad's moving to town."

His world tilted off-axis. How could it be that the first time he kissed this woman— the first time he felt like they were on track for something more—that her ex came back into the picture?

"I should go." He took a quick step back.

Livy turned to look at him. "I... yes... probably."

He'd wanted Livy to assure him that no, he

should stay. So much for that hope. It shattered with her words.

"I'll walk you out." She led him back to the front door and opened it.

He stood in the doorway, not knowing what to say. Wanting to kiss her goodbye but feeling awkward doing that with her ex sitting in the next room. The ex that still called her by her pet name, Livs.

"I'll see you soon," he said.

She stood and searched his face for a moment, then nodded. "Yes. Okay."

He turned and walked away.

Yes?

Okay?

What did that mean?

CHAPTER 21

Olivia walked back into the kitchen, her whole world spinning crazily out of control. And she *hated* feeling out of control. Austin had kissed her, and it had rocked her very being with the emotions that had careened through her. But she didn't have time to process all her thoughts about that just yet. Not now. Not with Brett sitting in her house.

And Brett was moving back to town? Why? She frowned. He always claimed he didn't want to be tied down to one place. Loved his traveling around all the time.

"Mom, isn't it great?" Emily was back sitting beside Brett, who was sipping on a beer like he belonged here.

He didn't.

"So you're moving to town?"

"I am. Decided I was tired of being so far away from my family."

By his family, she hoped he meant Emily. Because she, herself, was *not* his family. Never had been.

"So, who was that guy?" he asked like it was any of his business.

"A friend."

"He's the guy who's been helping me learn all that techie stuff I was telling you about. We set up online ordering for the cafe," Emily explained.

Brett frowned. "You're going to do online ordering? Didn't you just open? Can you handle all that?"

Thanks for the support, Brett. But she didn't say that out loud. She ignored it. "You have a job here?"

"Not yet, but I've sent out a lot of feelers. Have a few nibbles. Don't worry, Livs, I'm sure I'll find something soon." He sat back in his chair, in control, sure the world would drop into place for him like it always did.

Like how he was so relieved when she

agreed they shouldn't get married when she got pregnant and that she'd raise Emily alone. He was free to move on.

Which he did. Immediately. Before Emily was even born.

Why now, after all these years, did he feel the need to come and be a part of Emily's life?

So, all she said was, "I see." But she didn't see. She was confused. He had some hotshot job that kept him traveling all over. To be honest, she wasn't sure exactly what he did these days. Just knew he rarely visited Emily... and now he was going to *live* here? In Moonbeam?

She walked to the fridge and pulled out a beer for herself. Because *she did* belong here. She leaned against the counter and took a sip, looking over at the pair of them. Emily's eyes danced with delight at having Brett here. And that made her happy. It did. She just didn't want to deal with Brett right now. Or have things get more complicated. Or... different.

"So where are you staying?"

"I'm at The Cabot Hotel for a few days. Looking for an apartment to rent." He flashed her a boyish smile. A familiar one, but one that had no effect on her now. Not like it had all those years ago. But Brett was a charmer. Always had been. Always would be. And he was Emily's father, so she better get used to having him around. For Emily's sake.

She looked at her watch. "It's getting late. Emily, you should be getting ready for bed soon." As if she determined Emily's bedtime any more.

She looked pointedly at Brett.

"Oh, I should go then," he said as he took the last swig of his beer and got to his feet. "Night, Emily. See you tomorrow."

Tomorrow? But she better get used to that if he was moving back. He'd probably be seeing Emily a lot. She'd have to learn to share their daughter. She glanced over at Emily, who still looked like she'd gotten everything single thing she wanted on an enchanted Christmas morning.

Brett left his bottle on the table and headed for the front door. He never had been one to pick up after himself. She glared at the bottle, swiped it up, and tossed it into the recycling bin.

"Mom, isn't this just so cool?" Emily popped up from the table and hugged her. "I'll have both parents in the same town. So cool." With that, she twirled out of the kitchen and headed to her room. Olivia smiled in spite of herself. Who didn't love to see their child that happy?

Olivia took her beer, went outside, and sank onto a chair in the moonlight. Not exactly how she thought this evening would end. After that kiss, she'd hoped to sit out here with Austin. Kiss him again. Hold hands. Talk and laugh.

All she could see was the image of Brett and Emily, laughing at the table, her daughter so happy.

And Brett's nickname for her. Livs. That was from years ago when they'd been... intimate. Close. He had no place using it anymore. They were barely friends. Just Emily's parents. That's all they shared now.

At first, she'd sent him lots of photos of Emily. Cute drawings she did as she got older. Tracked him down in Europe one time when Emily had gotten really sick and they'd had quite a scare. But he hadn't come back then. He rarely showed up to visit, though he did call Emily once in a while. Emily adored him and craved any attention he gave to her.

Maybe this would work out okay? She never wanted to keep Emily from Brett. But this had all come on so suddenly, and it was so like Brett not to give her a heads up.

She looked up at the stars, searching for answers and hoping they'd give her strength or a clue on how to learn to live with Brett back in their lives.

CHAPTER 22

"What's wrong with you today?" Heather asked Olivia as she passed by her in the cafe, a bin of dirty dishes tucked against her hip. "You gave table two table one's order. And you're not stopping and chatting with people. You okay?"

Olivia sighed. "I'm... fine."

"Right." Heather rolled her eyes. "We'll talk after the crowd dies down."

Sure enough, Heather came and found her in the kitchen as the breakfast crowd waned. "So, tell me what's going on."

Olivia sank into a chair. "Guess who's back in town."

"I have no clue." Heather grabbed the chair across from her. "Who?"

"Brett."

"Really? He hasn't visited in a long time."

"Yes, well, this isn't a visit. He's moving to Moonbeam."

Heather's eyes flew open wide. "Moving here? But... why?"

"He said he wanted to be closer to his... *family*."

"You mean closer to Emily." Heather frowned.

"I'm just repeating what he said. He's planning on getting an apartment. He has no job here yet though. And as near as I can figure he's planning on seeing Emily all the time." She shrugged. "Which, I get it. Emily is excited to have him here. I'm happy for her. I'm just not used to... sharing her. That sounds terrible, doesn't it?"

Heather reached over and squeezed her hand. "No, it doesn't sound terrible. It sounds normal. It will be a big adjustment having him here."

"I just don't know how it will all work out. When he gets a place, will he want her to stay there some? Is he going to start voicing opinions on what she does? Where she's thinking of going to college? I'm used to raising her alone. Making decisions on my own."

"You guys will work it out. It just might take a bit." Heather leaned forward and frowned. "And... what else is bothering you?"

She let out a short laugh. "Ah, you know me so well. It seems that Brett couldn't have planned his return at a more unfortunate time."

"Why's that?" Heather's brow quirked up questioningly.

"So after Austin walked me home?" She felt a blush sweep across her cheeks. "He... he kissed me."

"Well, good for him."

"It was... nice. Very nice. I asked him inside. Thought we might have a drink out on the lanai."

Heather grinned.

"But then we went inside and there was Brett, sitting at the kitchen table with Emily, and acting like he belonged there."

"That was some lousy timing."

"Austin couldn't get out of there fast enough. I can't blame him. It was just... awkward."

"I'm sure he'll pop by today and talk to you. You two can sort that out, too. Sounds like you have a lot of sorting out to do." Heather laughed. "And you hate feeling out of control."

"I do." She grimaced. "I so hate it."

HEATHER WALKED into Aunt Donna's house the next evening and saw her mother sitting at the table with papers spread before her, a pen in hand.

"Mother, what are you doing?"

"I'm signing the divorce papers." Her mother looked up with a determined set to her lips.

"But why? I thought you were going to stall after Father ordered you to sign them?"

"I was... but then I realized... I *do* want to sign them. I'm done being married to him. I want it all over. To move on. I'm just over it."

"But he'll get what he wants, and he's not giving you anything. Nothing at all." Heather frowned, not understanding this move her mother was making. She thought her mother would fight, would push back, demand some kind of settlement. Not just... give up.

"But I *am* getting something." Her mother's eyes flashed. "I'm getting my freedom. And I don't plan on ever letting anyone tell me what to do or how to live my life, ever again."

Heather turned at the sound of Donna and Livy entering the kitchen. "Hey, what are you two up to?" Livy asked.

"Mother is signing the divorce papers."

Donna's eyebrows rose. "Are you, Evie?" Donna crossed over and sat down beside her sister. "Are you sure that's what you want to do?"

"I'm positive."

Donna paused, then nodded. "Then sign away. I'm one hundred percent behind any decision you make."

Evelyn hugged Donna. "Thank you. I appreciate that."

Livy came to stand beside Heather. "You okay with this?" she whispered.

"I am if Mother is." Or at least she thought she was. If this is what her mother truly wanted, it was the right thing to do. It did irritate her that it meant that her father was getting what he'd commanded. But if it was what her mother wanted, that was what was important.

Donna looked up from where Evelyn was signing the papers and saw their mother standing in the doorway to the kitchen. She groaned inwardly. The timing couldn't be any worse. The last thing Evelyn needed was her mother's criticism right now.

"So, you're all here." Patricia walked into the room.

"What are doing here, Grandmother?" Olivia stepped up, partially hiding the kitchen table.

"I had my driver bring me to town to see that new retirement complex. As you know, I've been very upset at the lack of upkeep at the complex I'm at in Naples. They just aren't keeping things as nice as they should. Some of the ladies are considering Sunrise Village here in Moonbeam."

"So you toured it? Did you like it?" Donna rose and stood beside Olivia. She could hear Evelyn gathering the papers behind her. Good plan. No use letting their mother know what was going on.

"It was beautifully kept up. The rooms are fairly nice, especially if you get one of their upgraded suites, which of course I would."

"So, you're moving back to Moonbeam?"

Heather walked over until they had a solid three-woman hedge blocking Evelyn and her papers from Patricia.

"I'm not certain. But possibly. I'm going to talk to some of my friends back at our place in Naples. But I just cannot stay where I am. It's just not... good enough anymore." A frown creased Patricia's face. "Such a shame. It was supposed to be the best of the best. And really, Moonbeam doesn't have the social activities and cultural opportunities that Naples has."

Evelyn came around from behind the table. "I'm sure you'll make the right decision, whatever you decide."

"I'm sure I will." Their mother looked surprised that anyone would even question whether she'd make a wrong decision. Which was kind of rich, considering how often their mother questioned their decisions.

"So, what's this I heard about that man coming back to town?"

"What man?" Olivia asked nervously.

"Your man. That man that got you pregnant. Is it even proper for him to be back in town? It's just going to bring up all the old gossip."

"Grandmother, he's Emily's father. He has every right to move here to be by her."

Donna looked over at her daughter, proud of the way she was standing up to her grandmother.

"It just doesn't seem... proper... to me. If I move back here to Moonbeam, we can't have rumors going around. You girls are going to have to make sure that you do things properly. Make sure there isn't gossip floating around town. If my friends move here too... well, we can't have gossip. We cannot. I won't stand for it."

Donna looked over at Evelyn, then back at their mother. "I'm sure it will be fine, Mother. And you haven't even decided yet, have you?"

"No, not for certain. I'll need to see which ladies are planning on moving here first."

Of course. Make sure the *proper* people were moving to Sunrise Village. Of course. Donna looked at her mother, knowing she should ask her to come and sit down and offer her some tea. But suddenly she was tired. And a half-hour of listening to her mother condemn the town or things any of them did just seemed like thirty minutes too long.

Her mother glanced at the gold watch

dangling from her wrist. "Well, I can't stay. It's getting late. My driver is waiting for me in the drive."

"Okay, Mom. Glad you stopped by." Suddenly Donna wasn't quite as tired as she led her mother back to the front door.

Her mother stepped outside, then turned back to her. "I mean it, Donna. You must make sure that you keep everyone under control if I move back here. No gossip. No scandal."

She just nodded as her mother walked away, and her driver held the door open for her. She settled into the back seat and they drove away.

"Bye, Mother," she whispered softly.

What kind of daughter was hoping that her mother *didn't* move to town? That she found another place a safe distance away? She sighed as she went back inside.

She found the three of them opening a bottle of red wine. She laughed. "I guess this does call for a drink."

"To surviving Mother's visit?" Evelyn grinned.

Donna laughed. "No, we're going to toast to your newfound freedom." She raised her glass. "To Evelyn. May her life be filled with happiness from this day forward."

"To Evelyn," Heather and Olivia toasted.

"And to the strong Parker women. Every one of us."

And the Parker women all clinked their glasses.

CHAPTER 23

By the middle of the week, they'd discovered that Melody Tanner was an excellent cook, too. She became a great help to Evelyn in the kitchen. Olivia hired Brittany, a friend of Emily's, to work after school and on Saturdays. She was still toying with the idea of hiring another person full-time, but for now Heather was helping them out each day. She kept thinking that their rush of customers would slow down as the newness of the cafe wore off.

Or maybe not.

Austin hadn't been in yet this week. Or called. She'd half-expected him to ask her out again for Sunday since he knew the cafe was closed on Sundays. But her phone had been silent.

"Hey, you."

She whirled around at the sound of Austin's voice. *Had just thinking about him made him appear?*

No, because she'd been thinking about him nonstop since Sunday night**...**

"Hi, Austin." Her heart fluttered in her chest at the sight of him. At the memory of his kisses.

"Thought I'd come in and grab some supper. You look really busy, though."

She glanced around the crowded room. "We are, but take that table over there. I'll get you a menu."

She went to get him a menu and deliver an order to a table. Then, as she was headed to take his order, she paused. There were Emily and Brett sitting just two tables from Austin with Brittany taking their order. Emily waved to her, a happy look plastered on her face at eating dinner with her father.

She went to Austin's table and saw that he'd noticed Emily and Brett. "Emily looks happy," Austin said.

"She does. She's enjoying having Brett around." She took out the order pad and a pen. "You ready to order?"

"I think I'll have the meatloaf sandwich."

"Good choice." She nodded, all the while feeling like Brett was watching her every move. Which was silly.

"And I think I'll have a vanilla malt to go with it." Austin glanced over at Emily and Brett's table as he handed her the menu.

"I'll have your order out to you soon." She turned and headed to the kitchen.

Heather looked up as she entered. "You okay?"

"Yes, it's just... Austin came in. And we're crazy busy, so I can't really talk to him. And... Emily and Brett are here eating dinner, too. And Brett is... watching me. Or maybe I'm imagining that."

"If Emily has told him about Austin, maybe he's jealous?"

"Why would he be jealous?"

"Because Brett didn't want to be married to you or have the responsibility of raising Emily... but then, I'm not sure he's ever gotten over you."

"That makes no sense." She shook her head.

"Okay, but I still think he has a thing for you."

"That's crazy."

"Whatever you say..." Heather rolled her

eyes, then handed her another order. "Table Six."

She went back out into the dining room and delivered the order, then made the malt for Austin and brought it to his table.

"I guess you're too busy to sit down for a bit?" he asked.

"Yes, I'm sorry. We're just crazy busy tonight."

"But being busy is good, right?"

"Right." She glanced over and caught Brett staring at her. She ignored it. Mostly. "I'll go check on your order."

She headed back to the kitchen, grabbed Austin's order, and dropped it off at his table.

"Thanks." He smiled at her and her heart did that little flip again.

She was tempted to sit down with him if only for a minute...

"Mom." Emily waved and motioned her over to their table.

"Better go see what she wants." Austin tilted his head toward Emily.

She nodded and headed over to Emily and Brett's table. "Hi, honey. Enjoying your dinner?"

"Evelyn's meatloaf is like the best ever," Emily said.

"Have to agree with our daughter on that one," Brett added. "Can you sit down and join us for a bit?"

"Can you, Mom?"

She looked around the room. "I wish I could. But all the tables are full and we're so busy."

"Just for a minute. I have something to tell you." Emily pulled out the chair beside her.

Okay, if Emily needed to tell her something, then the customers would have to wait just a minute. She sank into the chair.

"So... Dad and I have been talking. When school is out, he's talking about taking me to Paris. Paris! Can you imagine?"

She sat there stunned for a moment. "France?"

"That's usually where Paris is." Brett gave her that boyish grin of his.

"Doesn't that sound wonderful? I've always wanted to go there." Emily's eyes sparkled with excitement.

"Well... we'll have to talk about it."

"Why?" Emily frowned. "I want to go. I'll be with Dad. It will be great."

She looked over at Brett. How could he just decide he was going to do this without even discussing it with her? "We'll talk about it later. I really need to get back to work."

"I'm going," Emily stated the fact as if the decision was hers to make.

"We'll, see you back at the house, then," Brett said as if it was *his* house.

So far he'd been over at *her* house every night this week. But then, it was Emily's house, too. And Brett was her father. But he couldn't just make a big decision like taking Emily out of the country without even checking with her. She stood up. "Okay, I'll see you at home. And Brett, we need to talk."

She turned and hurried over to a table of new customers, took their order and another table's, and went into the kitchen.

"You okay? You looked ticked off," Heather said as she handed her an order to deliver.

"No, I'm not okay. Not in the least bit. Brett has told Emily he's taking her to Paris."

"Without even talking to you first?"

"Right. I'm just so..." She paused and counted to three. Then five. "I've got to get back to work. But you know what? I am going to hire someone else to work here. I have to be able to spend more time with Emily."

"Good plan. I think you do need more help here."

Melody walked over to them. "Did you say you need more help? I can work more hours. I'd love to work full time instead of part time."

"That will help. Are you sure?" Maybe Melody could even take over some of the cooking so that Evelyn could have some time off. If Evelyn taught her how to make the recipes.

"I'm sure."

"Perfect. But I'm still going to consider hiring even more help if things don't slow down by next week. And Heather, you need to get back to your art. You can't fill in here forever."

"I don't mind."

"I know, but you have your career. I just need to find someone responsible."

With that decision made, she headed back out to the dining room. She glanced over at Austin's table and it was empty. Brittany walked past her. "He left. I checked him out for you."

"Oh... okay, thanks." But she had to admit her feelings were a bit hurt that he'd left without saying anything to her. Though she had been crazy busy. And gotten tied up in the kitchen for a bit helping plate some orders. She fought off the disappointment that swept through her. She'd asked him out the last time... and now she felt like it was his move. He should ask her out if he was interested in dating her.

But then, maybe he wasn't...

CHAPTER 24

Austin walked out of the cafe. He probably should have waited and said something to Livy. But she was busy. And then she'd sat down and chatted with Emily and her ex after saying she was too busy to sit down with him. The writing was on the wall.

And the three of them had looked like they were having a serious discussion. They'd looked all the world like a family having dinner together.

His timing was lousy. Supremely lousy.

He scowled as he walked along the sidewalk and back toward the hotel. He'd been briefly toying with finding an apartment here in Moonbeam. Working from here for a bit. He'd really come to like the small town. There was really nothing tying him down to Colorado.

But now it looked like he'd just be in the way.

He changed course and headed to the marina. Maybe Jesse would go get a beer with him after he brought The Destiny in. The boat was just docking as he got there. He waited until all the people disembarked, then climbed aboard. "Hey, Jesse. Got time for a beer?"

"Sure, just give me a minute. I'll have my deckhand get everything secure for the night."

Jesse came back in a few minutes. "Okay, where to?"

"Anywhere but Parker's Cafe." He scowled.

Jesse grinned. "You better not let Livy hear you call it that. She keeps insisting it's Sea Glass Cafe."

"I'd have to be able to actually talk to her to say it to her."

Jesse frowned. "What are you talking about? I thought you two had decided to date. Didn't you just go out on Sunday?"

"We did. And we had a great time. Well, *I* had a great time. But now her ex is back in town."

"Brett? He's not anything to Livy except for being Emily's father."

"Doesn't look that way to me."

"That's nuts."

"No, really. I think I should just step back. Give her space. Brett is moving back to town."

"Really? Moving to Moonbeam? That's... strange. He's never been that involved in Emily's life before."

"I don't know. But I didn't miss the way he looked at Livy. Maybe there's something still between them. And I don't want to get in the way of that. I mean, there's Emily to consider."

"Maybe. But I just never thought so. Didn't think he was right for her. I mean, the guy left her when she was pregnant. I know it was a mutual decision to not get married... but then he didn't even stick around to help."

"Well, he's back now."

Jesse slapped him on the back. "Come on, buddy. Let's go have that beer. I'm buying."

They headed to Jimmy's with Austin's heart cracking a bit with each step. Which was crazy because he hadn't known Livy that long. Maybe three or so weeks now? Four? And he'd only kissed her that one night. He was just being ridiculous.

~

Olivia walked home after closing the cafe. She was overwhelmingly tired. Maybe from the long, hard day. Maybe because of the strangeness of having Brett around. She walked into her house, readying herself for the confrontation that she knew was coming.

Emily was sitting by herself at the kitchen table, working on schoolwork. "Hey, Ems. Where's your dad?"

"He had to leave."

More likely he was avoiding her because she said they needed to talk. She pulled out her phone to text him.

He didn't answer.

Fine. But she was going to keep texting him until he did.

"Mom, you're going to let me go to Paris with Dad, aren't you?" Emily looked up from her homework.

"We'll talk about it. I'd have to know details. You'd need a passport, you know."

"I know. I'm going to go get a passport photo taken tomorrow. Please say I can go."

"I need to talk to your father first. If you want my answer right this minute, it's no."

Emily shut her textbook and stood up. "No, I'll wait. But I really, *really* want to go. Like really." Emily went to her room, and Olivia puttered around the house. Emptying the dishwasher, taking out the trash, throwing a load of laundry in.

She texted Brett again and said she needed to talk to him.

This time he answered her and said he could meet her tomorrow night. He suggested Jimmy's at eight. That would work for her, so she replied yes. She'd leave work a tiny bit early and head to the pier. Then she and Brett were going to have to figure out this whole co-parenting thing. And it didn't involve suggesting trips across the world without discussing it first.

CHAPTER 25

Barry stopped by The Cabot Hotel when he got back to Moonbeam on Friday. Delbert had said that he wanted to see him.

Barry had known almost right away that the new job in Oregon wasn't going to be a good fit for him. The owner was a micromanager for one thing. And he was pretty sure the man didn't like any of the suggestions he'd made. He wasn't expecting a job offer on that one. But he would have to find one soon. Still, he had to admit he was a bit relieved that he wouldn't be all the way across the country with a new job.

He poked his head into Delbert's office. "Hey, how are things going here? Did that replacement furniture ever arrive?"

"Welcome back. Yes, the order came in.

How did your interview go?" Delbert stood and came around from the back of his desk.

"It didn't. It just wasn't a good fit. Hey, can't expect everyone to be as great to work for as you were."

Delbert grinned. "Glad to hear you say that."

"What, that I didn't get the job?"

"Precisely. Because I have a proposition for you. So this week I just closed the deal on an old hotel near Naples. I didn't think they'd take my offer, but the other person bidding on it pulled out. It's quite rundown, but in its prime it was really grand. I want to restore it like we did The Cabot. You interested in running point on this one from the very beginning?"

"You're offering me another job?"

"I am. It's a little less than an hour away. You could stay down there… or, you know… commute." Delbert grinned. "If there's any reason you'd like to be sticking around Moonbeam."

"I'll take it." He didn't even need to see the place. If Del thought it was a good hotel to restore, then it was. Relief and gratitude swept through him. He could stay here in Moonbeam. Be near Donna. This was just perfect.

Delbert smiled. "It's probably going to take at least a year for the project. You got that kind of time?"

"I have all the time in the world." He could feel the goofy smile on his face. This solved everything. A job. And staying near Donna.

"What are you waiting for? Don't you have someone you want to go see?" Delbert's mouth curved into a smile of satisfaction.

"Thanks, Del. I really appreciate this."

"My pleasure. You did a great job here. I'm sure you'll do a fabulous job there. We'll go down and see it next week. Make plans. Go over budgets."

"Sounds great. Can't wait." And with that, he hurried out of the hotel. He couldn't wait to find Donna and tell her the news. His heart beat in double-time just thinking of how surprised she'd be.

DONNA OPENED the door to find Barry standing there. He swooped her up in his arms, swung her around, then set her back down.

He laughed, then kissed her, then laughed

again. "I've missed you." His eyes shone with happiness.

But not any happier than she was to have him here again. Her heart fluttered just seeing him here in front of her. "I've missed you too. Come on in. Let's go sit out on the point."

She poured them some lemonade and led him out to the chairs on the point, anxious to hear about his week. And when he would be leaving... The euphoria from seeing him again began to ebb slowly away. Because he did have to leave. Start a new job. And if he got this one all the way across the country? What were they going to do?

She sank into her chair, took a sip of lemonade, and squared her shoulders, gathering strength. "So... how did the interview go?"

"Great. I didn't get the job."

She looked at him questioningly.

"It was a bad fit for me. Couldn't stand the owner of the company. And it... well, it wasn't right."

"So now you're back to looking for a job?"

"Nope." A wide grin spread across his face. "Got one. Just this afternoon, as a matter of fact."

"Really? Where?" She steeled herself for his answer and sucked in a quick breath.

"Here. Well, not here-here. But just south of here, near Naples. I'm going to stay in Moonbeam. It seems I've become fond of the place." He reached out and took her hand. "And fond of the people here."

Her heart leapt, and joy flooded through her. "You're staying here? In Moonbeam?" She wanted to make sure she'd heard him correctly.

"At least for another year or so, yes." He stood up and pulled her to her feet. "You're happy about that, aren't you?"

"Very." Her heart skittered as she looked up at him.

"Good, because you see..." He paused and searched her face. "It seems I've come to love you."

"You do?" Her voice squeaked.

"Yes, I do, Donna. Very much." He leaned close and kissed her gently.

"That's... nice that you do."

He stood there staring at her.

"I mean, it's really nice." Why wouldn't her words work? Why couldn't she tell him she loved him? It was plain that he was standing there waiting for her words. Instead, she turned and walked over to the edge of the patio out on the point. She stood there silently watching the water slip past in the waterway. She was so happy to hear his words. To hear that he loved her. But she just couldn't give him what he wanted to hear in return.

He came up behind her and wrapped his arms around her waist. "That's okay. You don't have to say anything. I know I just kind of sprung all this on you. Staying here in Moonbeam. Telling you how I feel."

She spun around in his arms and looked up into his warm eyes. "It's just... I do care about you. I do." But the men in her life that she'd cared about left her. Every one of them. If she told him she loved him, would that just lead to him leaving her, too? It sounded silly in her mind, but it was how she felt.

"Donna, there is no pressure. And if you'd rather me move down near Naples than stay next door, I can do that too. The last thing I want to do is pressure you into something you're not ready for."

"No, don't leave." That was precisely what she didn't want to happen. She reached out and grabbed both his hands. "I'm glad you're staying here. Very glad. I missed you so much this week. I've gotten used to seeing you almost every day. And I've missed your company. Talking to you. Just sitting with you."

"I missed you, too."

"And I'm glad you told me how you feel. I'm just not ready... I can't..." She sighed. "Just give me some time."

"I'll give you as long as you need."

They sat back down and sipped lemonade in silence. Each of them lost in their thoughts. She wished she would have been able to tell him that she loved him, too.

But did she?

She cared deeply about him, but was that the same thing?

Or was she just too afraid to let herself take that last step and admit she was in love with him...

CHAPTER 26

Brett waved to Olivia as she came out on the deck at Jimmy's. She wove her way through the tables and sat down across from him.

"Hey, Livs, I ordered you your favorite beer. At least Emily said it was your favorite."

She had the wildest thought to refuse it and ask for wine because she couldn't stand him making decisions for her, even if it was only what she was going to drink. But she really wanted the beer. She reached across the table and took the bottle, pouring it into the frosty glass waiting for her.

"So, how is Parker's Cafe going? You look pretty busy." Brett gave her that boyish smile of his, then took a sip of his beer.

"Sea Glass Cafe," she corrected him. "Sea. Glass. Cafe. I don't know why everyone has such a hard time with that."

"Oh, sorry," he said. But he sure didn't look sorry.

"Brett, we need to talk."

"About what?" He threw her an innocent look.

"About you telling Emily that you'd take her to Paris without even discussing it with me first."

"But she loves history. She'll love it there. So much old stuff."

"Old stuff?" She eyed him.

"You know, museums and buildings and stuff. History."

"She doesn't even have a passport."

"We'll get her one." He set down his beer. "So, what's the problem?"

"A big decision like this... traveling halfway around the world. It should be discussed. Considered. You can't tell her you're taking her without asking me first."

He leaned forward. "So, tell me, Livs... would you have asked me if you decided to take Emily to Paris?"

"I—" She frowned. "No. But that's different. I've raised her. I've been there every step of the way with her. You've been**...**" She stared directly at him. "Not there."

"I want to be there for her now."

"But you can't just take her away." She refused to see his point. Even if he'd been right that she wouldn't have asked him. Heck, she and Emily might have gone to Paris and back and never *mentioned* it to him.

"I'm her parent, too. I want to take her to Paris. And you should come with us. We'd all have a great time. As a family."

She set her beer down carefully and stared across the table at him. What in the world was he suggesting?

Austin walked into Jimmy's planning on grabbing a quick beer. He'd been restless today. Wanting to call Livy and talk to her. But unsure. Uncertain. Maybe she wanted to try again with that Brett guy.

Anyway, a cold beer might soothe his nerves. He threaded his way through the crowd, sat at the bar outside, and ordered his now favorite beer—Livy's favorite local craft beer. So much had changed so quickly for him. He thought about her all the time. Which kind of annoyed him. But her laugh and her twinkling eyes and that smile of hers... He couldn't quit thinking about all of that.

Nor could he forget their kiss...

He grabbed the beer the bartender handed him, swept his gaze around the restaurant, and froze.

There sat Livy and Brett at the far side of the deck. Talking intently. He pulled his gaze away but then couldn't help himself, and he looked over again.

Livy had leaned forward, an earnest look on her face. And Brett looked... enraptured. Sure of himself.

Just then Brett leaned forward and took Livy's hands in his.

Austin had enough. He threw some bills down on the bar, took one more swig of his beer, setting it down on the bar with more force than intended. He spun around, not wanting to see anymore, and stalked off the deck in the opposite direction.

He'd had enough. He knew what he had to do.

It was time to leave Moonbeam.

CHAPTER 27

Livy's eyes widened as Brett reached out and grasped her hands across the table. She jerked her hands out of his grasp.

"What are you doing?"

"I'm trying to get you to listen to reason."

"I have been listening. Have you?"

"Come on, Livs." He gave her another of his famous boyish grins. It did nothing for her. She was way too angry at this point.

How had she ever fallen for this man all those years ago? Oh, she'd been young and foolish. But now her life was forever entwined with him because of Emily, whether she liked it or not.

She cocked her head and frowned. "Brett, why did you move back here?"

He sat back, surprised at the question. He chewed his lower lip for a moment. "Because Emily has been going on and on about this Austin guy this, Austin that. How great he is about teaching her things. How he's dating you. It's like he stepped into the place that I should be."

Shock washed over her in a cold wave of frigid clarity. "You didn't come back here thinking that... you don't think..." She sat back. "We're not getting back together. You know that, right? That's not what you want."

"I... I think we should give us another try. For Emily's sake."

Of course, he'd play his newfound daughter card. Classic Brett.

"Brett, we're not going to—as you put it —try again. You left me alone to raise Emily."

"But—"

She held up a hand to stop him. "You said we weren't a good match. That we shouldn't get married. We weren't a good match. We still aren't. But I didn't expect you to disappear from her life for months at a time. Do you know that one time you didn't call or reach out to her for eleven months? She kept track of it."

He looked at her in surprise. "She did?"

"Yes, you hurt her. A lot. And now, well, now you're back." And how long would that last?

"But Emily is our daughter. And I'm in Moonbeam now. Don't you think it just makes sense to see what's still between us?"

"There is nothing between us. Just Emily. She'll always be our daughter. But I'm not going to give us a try again—you and me. It's not happening. I don't feel that way about you."

"But you could try."

"No, I can't. I won't. Brett, I'm a different person than that young college girl. I've raised a child. I have my own business to run."

"So you're saying I don't fit in your life anymore?"

"Brett, you've never *wanted* to fit in my life."

"I do now."

"Why? Because I'm seeing someone? Someone who Emily likes?"

"It's like you and Emily have just moved on..."

She didn't miss the sadness in his eyes.

"No, it's always been Emily and me. The *two* of us."

Brett stood, the sadness in his eyes replaced with a flash of anger. "Okay, this whole thing has been a mistake. I thought if I moved back here, you'd give us a try."

"I thought you moved back here to be closer to Emily?" She eyed him warily.

"I think I'll just move on. It's obvious you don't want me here."

"Brett, let me make this as clear as possible. I do *not* want to date you. You are more than welcome to stay in Moonbeam and spend time with your daughter. I'll never do anything to get in between you two. But you and me? There isn't and won't be a you and me."

"Got it, Livs. Loud and clear." He spun around and walked away.

She slumped back in her chair. Well, that had been one confusing, emotional conversation.

CHAPTER 28

Donna perched on a stool in the kitchen at the cafe, sipping coffee with Evelyn.

"So, Barry is staying here in Moonbeam?" Evelyn asked.

"Yes, he is. For at least a year or so."

"That's fabulous news." Evelyn frowned. "So... why don't you look happy about it?"

"Because... Because he told me he loves me."

Evelyn laughed. "Of course he does. It's obvious to anyone who sees the way he looks at you. But you didn't tell him you love him, did you?"

"No... I didn't. I couldn't."

Evelyn jumped up and hugged her then pulled back, looking directly into her eyes. "Not all men are like Father and leave. Not all men are like Charlie and leave. They aren't even like Olivia's Brett."

"Or Darren?" She raised an eyebrow at her sister. "That's about all the men that have been involved with the Parker women, you know."

"How about Grace Parker and her husband? Or our grandmother and grandfather? Those were long-lasting relationships."

She nodded begrudgingly.

"But I refuse to think that it's all there is. That you shouldn't take a chance with Barry. He's a wonderful man. Kind. Funny. Hardworking. And he adores you. That's obvious. He's different than Father. We knew he didn't want to be a dad or spend time with us since we were little girls. It's different with Barry. He *wants* to be with you."

She pursed her lips. "He does. And I do like spending time with him."

"Then what's the problem. You love him, don't you?"

She stood there, still as a statute as she let the question sink in.

Did she love Barry?

She thought about their times together. The

fun times. The quiet times. How easy it was to be with him. The way her heart did double beats each time she saw him. Why hadn't it been obvious to her? Why had she let fear cause her to bury her feelings for him? He wasn't like any other man who had ever been in her life.

She gave Evelyn a reluctant smile. "Yes... I love him." She broke into a full grin. "I *love* him." Her heart sang with joy at saying it out loud.

Evelyn grinned and rolled her eyes. "I'm pretty sure that I'm not the one you should be saying it to."

She hugged her sister. "No, you're right. You're not. I've got to go find him."

"That sounds like the logical thing to do."

"I'll try his house. If he's not there, I'm going to track him down."

"Good luck." Evelyn's eyes twinkled with amusement.

She hurried across town, the whole time rehearsing what she'd say. How she'd tell him that she loved him. Deciding on the right words. She got to Barry's and paused on his front step, her hand raised, ready to knock. She took a deep breath, but before she could knock, the door swung open and Barry stood there, looking surprised. "Well, hello. I was just going to come over and visit you."

"Oh... I..." Suddenly she was nervous. She couldn't just say that she was coming over here to say that she loved him, could she?

"You okay?" He cocked an eyebrow.

"I'm fine. Perfect. I... I love you." And just like that, she blurted it out. Not exactly the way she'd planned, but she said it.

His smile spread into an easy grin. "That's nice to hear. Very nice." He pulled her into his arms.

"I do love you. It just took me a bit to sort it out and get up the nerve to say it."

"Loving a person can be a scary thing, huh?" He leaned back and looked into her eyes. "You give them the power to break your heart. But Donna, I won't break yours. I promise. And I won't leave. After this job is over in a year or so, we'll work something out. I'm not going anywhere. I'm not leaving you. Ever."

And those were just the words she needed to hear. She pressed her cheek against his chest, listening to his heart beat. And she knew she was right where she belonged.

CHAPTER 29

"Mom, what did you say to Dad?" Emily crashed through the front door of their house and raced into the kitchen.

"What are you talking about?"

"Dad is leaving."

"He is?"

"Yes, he said you don't want him here."

She looked at her daughter and took a deep, steadying breath. "I did not say that. I told him he was free to stay in Moonbeam so he could see you all the time."

"He said that you would make it too awkward to stay." Emily's eyes flashed defiantly. "I'm going to go to Paris with him this summer and we're going to stay a month. Maybe two."

"Emily—"

"No, Mom. I've had it. I'm old enough to make my own decisions. And I'll never forgive you for chasing Dad away. We could have finally been a family."

That hurt. Because she thought that she and Emily had been a family all along. For all these years.

Emily raced back through the house and slammed out the front door. Olivia stood, one hand on the counter. She needed a few moments to compose herself. Get her thoughts together. She'd wait until Emily calmed down and she'd talk to her. They'd always been able to talk. Always been honest with each other. They'd get through this like they'd always gotten through everything.

Wouldn't they?

But right now, it seemed like her whole life was crashing down around her.

She glanced around the empty kitchen. She needed to get out of here. A brisk walk might help. Maybe she'd even stop by Jimmy's and grab a drink. Listen to some music. Just give herself some time to unwind.

Standing here in the empty house with the

echoes of Emily's anger wasn't going to help. Jimmy's. A plan.

∼

HEATHER WALKED along the wharf that evening, too restless to go back to her apartment after helping out at the cafe. She kind of liked working there, even though she knew that soon Livy planned on replacing her with a permanent employee.

But right now, she felt like she belonged there at Parker's Cafe. She grinned to herself. *Sea Glass Cafe*.

She liked being here in the middle of the Parker women. She liked cooking beside her mother and hearing about Emily's day as she bubbled with excitement after school. Many nights she had a late dinner with her mother, Aunt Donna, and Livy after the cafe closed, sitting at a table near the counter, talking about their days. She'd never felt this strong a sense of... family.

And she liked it. She liked it a lot.

A smile crept across her face. To her utter delight, she saw Livy walking toward her. "Livy! Hey." She waved to her cousin.

Livy walked up to her. Heather could see immediately that she was upset. "What's wrong?"

"Everything. Nothing. Life." Livy shrugged.

"Want to go to Jimmy's and grab a quick drink?"

"That's where I was headed."

They grabbed a table by the water and ordered drinks. Heather looked across at Livy. "Okay, now tell me what's wrong."

"It's Brett. And Emily."

"So what happened?"

"Brett and I had a talk. I told him I wasn't happy about him telling Emily he'd take her to Paris without talking to me first. And then..." Livy paused while the server gave them their drinks. "Brett... he wanted us to try again. To date. To be a couple. Whatever."

"I told you he still had a thing for you." She sat back in triumph.

"I told him there was no way that was going to happen. I think..." She looked up at Heather. "I think he said he was going to move back here because Emily had been talking to him about Austin. You know, all the help he's been giving her with learning all the technical software programs. And then mentioned I was dating

Austin. So he decided he would move back here. Wants to be a family."

Heather took a sip of her drink and just let Livy continue to tell her what happened in her own time. She could see the turmoil clearly on Livy's face.

"Anyway, we can't be a family. We're not. And honestly, I don't trust him to not just disappear again." She let out a long sigh. "Which appears is exactly what he's doing. He's no longer going to move here."

"Well, that's good news, isn't it? Though Emily would like him here."

"He told Emily he wasn't going to move here because of me. That I wanted him to leave."

"What?" She set her drink down with a clatter. "You've never done one thing to stand between Brett and Emily. It's all his doing that he hasn't spent time with her."

"Emily is furious with me. And, no, I've never done anything to stand between her and Brett. And I told her I did *not* tell him to leave." A long breath escaped Livy. "I hate being on the outs with Emily. And I don't want to say anything to her that will hurt her relationship with Brett. Brett and my problems are just that. Problems between just him and me."

"Emily will calm down. She's a logical girl."

"And she says she's going to Paris with Brett. And they're going to stay for two months now."

Heather frowned. "Do you think that's really going to happen?"

"I don't know. He said that I should go to Paris with them. We should be a family. I think that's what he was planning all along."

"He does realize you are *not* a family? And then there's the little detail that you just opened Sea Glass Cafe."

"It's all just gotten so complicated."

"Brett has always been good at complicating your life. Remember Emily's sixth birthday? I came in town for it. Brett was supposed to come and said he was bringing her a big present. She stood by the window all day watching for him. And he never showed."

"And you slipped out and bought her the handheld game she'd been wanting and said it was from him." Livy shook her head. "Brett is full of disappointment and surprises."

"I'm sorry it's so hard right now."

Livy sat back. "And... just to add to things, Austin hasn't called. Hasn't asked me out again.

I don't know what's going on with him. It's like he kissed me and decided that he's not interested."

"Of course he's interested. Why don't you call him? You ask him out?"

"I did that last time."

"Do it again. Bet he says yes. Weren't you just telling me a few weeks ago to talk to Jesse to sort things out?"

"And did you?"

"No, but… that's different. You should go talk to Austin."

Livy slumped in her chair. "I don't know… and now with Brett and Emily. And the cafe opening. My life is just crazy right now."

"But you care about him, don't you? I can tell. I haven't seen you interested in someone in a very long time."

"I… I suppose I do care about him. But really, I've only known him, what, about a month or so?"

"And some people fall for each other the first time they lay eyes on one another. Anyway, why not ask him out? See what happens. Figure out how he feels. Sometimes you have to just take a risk and go after what you want. You did that with the cafe. You can do that with Austin."

"Maybe..." Livy sat up straight and grabbed her drink. "But I'm not making any promises."

"You know I'll keep bugging you until you do." Heather grinned.

Livy laughed. "I know you will."

CHAPTER 30

The next night Olivia came home to an empty house. Emily had texted that she was out with friends and would be home late. Whether that meant out with school friends or out with Brett, she didn't know. She wasn't even certain if Brett was still in town.

Between the long hours and the stress with Emily, it had been a long, long day. Austin hadn't come by the cafe, and she'd taken her phone out a half dozen times to text him but never quite followed through.

She reached for a pitcher of lemonade in the fridge and poured herself a large glass. Maybe she'd sit out on the lanai and just relax a bit.

The doorbell rang and she frowned. She

didn't usually have late visitors. She went to answer it and swung the door wide.

There stood Austin. Holding a bag. Looking ever so handsome and... distant.

"Do you have a minute?" he asked with an overly formal tone.

"Sure, come in." She led him to the kitchen. "I was just having some lemonade. Want some?"

"Uh... sure."

She poured him a glass and handed it to him, their fingers brushing slightly. She snapped her hand back as if it were on fire.

"So, I'm getting ready to leave town."

"You are?" She wasn't prepared for the sharp pain that surged through her.

"Yes, I think it's time to move on. I have most of my accounts here wrapped up to the point I can handle them from a distance." He thrust out the bag toward her. "But I wanted to give this to Emily. It's a book on computer coding. One of the best I've seen. I thought she might like it."

"That was nice of you." She took the bag and set it on the counter. "I'm sure she'll be sorry to see you go."

"I'll miss teaching her. She was a quick learner. You have a great daughter."

She knew that. And knew that eventually she and Emily would sort things out. They always did and she just hoped they did this time. The sooner, the better. "She is a great kid."

Austin stood there awkwardly looking around the kitchen, avoiding looking directly at her.

She screwed up her courage. "So... the other night. You kissed me."

He only nodded.

"And I thought that it meant something. I thought there might be something between us. The start of something." She shrugged with a little laugh. "Or... *something*."

He looked closely at her, then walked over and set his glass on the counter. "Listen, I know that Brett is back. That he's moving back here. That's great for Emily, right? And... I saw you and him at Jimmy's. He was holding your hands. I don't want to get in the middle of that. You have every right to give things a chance. Become a family. I'm just sorry our timing was so off." He gave her a small smile. "Because I did enjoy spending time with you. And the kiss *did* mean something to me."

"You saw me at Jimmy's? Why didn't you come over?"

"I didn't want to interrupt."

"You wouldn't have interrupted anything. And if you'd stayed, you would have seen me snatch my hands back. There is nothing between Brett and me."

He looked at her skeptically.

"You don't have to worry about Brett. He's... well, he's Emily's father, so he'll always be in our lives in some way. But that has nothing to do with me. I don't have feelings for him except his being Emily's dad."

He swept his gaze over her face as if searching to see if she was telling the truth.

And taking that risk, she plunged on. "I... I have feelings for you. I care about you."

"You do?" His eyes widened in astonishment.

"Yes, you foolish man."

His mouth spread into a wide grin. "That's just perfect, because I have feelings for you, too. I want to see where this is headed."

"So are you still leaving?" She cocked her head to one side.

"Not a chance." His eyes twinkled and he shook his head.

Suddenly her heart soared, and her world began to fall slowly back into place. She grinned up at him. "Then kiss me again. It's been too long."

And he did as happiness bubbled through her.

EPILOGUE

Early that summer Olivia sat at the table at her mother's house with Aunt Evelyn and Heather, sharing a bottle of wine. She'd finally hired some more help at the cafe and they occasionally took an evening off. She'd been surprised when the number of customers had never really dropped off after the opening and the cafe had begun to show a nice profit.

"So, I have some news." Aunt Evelyn looked around at all of them.

"What's that?" Donna asked.

"I've found an apartment. I'm moving out on my own." Evelyn's eyes shone with excitement. "I've never lived on my own and can't wait."

"Good for you." Olivia nodded. "I think that's great."

"I admit, I'm going to miss having you here," Donna said.

"Because of my cooking, right?" Evelyn smiled.

Donna laughed. "Your cooking *and* your company."

"I'll help you move, Mom," Heather offered.

"I'll take all the help I can get. I have to get some furniture too, but I'm in no hurry. Except for a bed. I want one of those." Evelyn laughed.

"And you have your cooking pots and pans," Heather said.

"We can look at that secondhand store that just reopened in town. It's supposed to have a lot of nice things at good prices," Olivia suggested.

"I think shopping will be fun. But I'm going to take my time. Only get things I really want."

"As opposed to buying what your interior decorator insisted you get at your house with Father?" Heather asked.

"Exactly. I never really did like her style, though everything looked nice. It just wasn't me."

"Now you'll have a chance to get exactly what you want." Donna got up from the table.

"I'm going to get us some cheese and crackers to go with our wine."

"So, have you heard from Emily since she left for Paris? It's been what, a week or so now?" Heather asked.

"Just one text saying she got there safely. But I made her promise to do that." She and Emily had still not gotten back on very good footing.

"Things still strained between you?" Aunt Evelyn gave her a sympathetic look.

"Better, but not back to how they were before."

"And that's Brett's fault. His lies to Emily." Heather frowned. "And the fact he said he was moving here to be near Emily... but then that never happened."

Just then her cell rang, and she snatched it out of her pocket. Her eyes widened when she saw the number. "Emily?"

"Mom..."

Her heart pounded at the tone. She immediately knew something was wrong. "What is it?"

"Mom, I'm so sorry. Sorry about everything."

"Emily, it's okay. We're okay. Don't worry about it. Just enjoy your time in Paris."

"Mom… do you think I could come home?"

She frowned. "Of course you can. What's wrong?"

"Everything. Dad met someone here and has been going out every night."

"And leaving you alone?"

"Mom, I'm fine."

"You're not going out alone in Paris at night, are you?" A flash of panic raced through her at the thought of her daughter roaming Paris streets alone.

"No. I bought some history books on Paris and I've been reading them at night."

Just like Brett to not even concentrate on spending time with his daughter when he had the chance.

"And… well… I figured out it wasn't your fault that he didn't move to Moonbeam. Just from things he said. Did he ask you to go out with him again, Mom?"

She paused, not knowing how to answer. Not wanting to involve Emily in things with Brett. But she couldn't lie. "Yes, he did."

"You know that he's not right for you though, don't you? He's just… not. He's my dad, but he's not…" Emily let out a long sigh. "He's not good enough to date you. He wouldn't treat you right. Not like Austin does. He's kind of... self-centered."

That daughter of hers was a smart young lady.

"So can I come home? I already looked up changing my tickets. If I do it now they are having a sale and it won't cost much more. I can work at the cafe this summer and save up more money for college."

"Of course you can come home and of course you can work at the cafe."

"Great. I'll be there the day after tomorrow."

"Perfect. Text me the info and I'll be at the airport to pick you up. I love you, Ems."

"Love you, Mom."

The connection broke, and she turned to see everyone smiling at her.

"So, Emily's coming home?" Heather asked.

"She is." Happiness swirled through her. Her Emily was coming home.

"That's perfect." Donna raised her glass, and they all joined in. "To all the Parker women back in one place again."

"To the Parker women," Olivia toasted as a wonderful feeling of peace and rightness flowed through her. The Parker women always seemed to come through everything that life threw at them.

Together.

There was nothing like family. And hers was the best.

Dear Reader,

I hope you enjoyed The Parker Cafe—I mean, the *Sea Glass Cafe*... LOL. Now it's time for Heather and Jesse's story. And wow, there are some secrets there! Get book three in the Moonbeam Bay series.

A HEATHER PARKER ORIGINAL

I had originally planned five books in the series, but in the process of writing—much to my surprise—I discovered there **has** to be a book six, too. Watch for more books in the Moonbeam Bay series coming soon!

Do you want to be the first to know about exclusive promotions, news, giveaways, and new releases? See the VIP READER signup on my website.

kaycorrell.com

Or join my reader group on Facebook. They're always helping name my characters, see my covers first, and we just generally have a good time.

www.facebook.com/groups/KayCorrell/

As always, thanks for reading my stories. I truly appreciate all my readers.

Happy reading,

Kay

ALSO BY KAY CORRELL

COMFORT CROSSING ~ THE SERIES

The Shop on Main - Book One

The Memory Box - Book Two

The Christmas Cottage - A Holiday Novella
(Book 2.5)

The Letter - Book Three

The Christmas Scarf - A Holiday Novella (Book 3.5)

The Magnolia Cafe - Book Four

The Unexpected Wedding - Book Five

The Wedding in the Grove (crossover short story
between series - Josephine and Paul from The
Letter.)

LIGHTHOUSE POINT ~ THE SERIES

Wish Upon a Shell - Book One

Wedding on the Beach - Book Two

Love at the Lighthouse - Book Three

Cottage near the Point - Book Four

Return to the Island - Book Five

Bungalow by the Bay - Book Six

CHARMING INN ~ Return to Lighthouse Point

One Simple Wish - Book One

Two of a Kind - Book Two

Three Little Things - Book Three

Four Short Weeks - Book Four

Five Years or So - Book Five

Six Hours Away - Book Six

Charming Christmas - Book Seven

SWEET RIVER ~ THE SERIES

A Dream to Believe in - Book One

A Memory to Cherish - Book Two

A Song to Remember - Book Three

A Time to Forgive - Book Four

A Summer of Secrets - Book Five

A Moment in the Moonlight - Book Six

MOONBEAM BAY ~ THE SERIES (2021)

The Parker Women - Book One (Jan 2021)

The Parker Cafe - Book Two (Feb 2021)

A Heather Parker Original - Book Three

The Parker Family Secret - Book Four

Grace Parker's Peach Pie - Book Five

The Perks of Being a Parker - Book Six

INDIGO BAY ~ Save by getting Kay's complete collection of stories previously published separately in the multi-author Indigo Bay series. The three stories are all interconnected.

Sweet Days by the Bay

Or buy them separately:

Sweet Sunrise - Book Three

Sweet Holiday Memories - A short holiday story

Sweet Starlight - Book Nine

ABOUT THE AUTHOR

Kay writes sweet, heartwarming stories that are a cross between women's fiction and contemporary romance. She is known for her charming small towns, quirky townsfolk, and enduring strong friendships between the women in her books.

Kay lives in the Midwest of the U.S. and can often be found out and about with her camera, taking a myriad of photographs which she likes to incorporate into her book covers. When not lost in her writing or photography, she can be found spending time with her ever-supportive husband, knitting, or playing with her puppies —two cavaliers and one naughty but adorable Australian shepherd. Kay and her husband also love to travel. When it comes to vacation time, she is torn between a nice trip to the beach or the mountains—but the mountains only get considered in the summer—she swears she's allergic to snow.

Learn more about Kay and her books at kaycorrell.com

While you're there, sign up for her newsletter to hear about new releases, sales, and giveaways.

WHERE TO FIND ME:
kaycorrell.com
authorcontact@kaycorrell.com

Join my Facebook Reader Group. We have lots of fun and you'll hear about sales and new releases first!
https://www.facebook.com/groups/KayCorrell/

I love to hear from my readers. Feel free to contact me at authorcontact@kaycorrell.com

- facebook.com/KayCorrellAuthor
- instagram.com/kaycorrell
- pinterest.com/kaycorrellauthor
- amazon.com/author/kaycorrell
- bookbub.com/authors/kay-correll

Made in United States
North Haven, CT
29 May 2024

53100447R10169